Guillermo N   n Bahia Blanca, Argentina, in 1962. Since 1985 he has lived in Buenos Aires, where he obtained a Ph.D. in Mathematical Science. He has written several highly acclaimed novels and books of short stories. *The Oxford Murders*, which was awarded the prestigious Planeta prize, is the first of his works to be published in the UK and has been made into a major film starring Elijah Wood.

Praise for *The Oxford Murders*:

'The mix of mathematics and murder mystery makes for a powerful cocktail. *The Oxford Murders* is not the first thriller to combine the two, but it is one of the first to do it successfully . . . there is a lightness of touch in the way the themes are laid out in the book that makes it a very easy read. Although the fast-paced narrative compels one to gobble up the story, the mathematician in me wanted to hold back to crack the problem before I was told the solution. In the end the solution is unexpected yet perfectly logical and watertight – just like the best bits of mathematics'

Guardian

'Guillermo Martínez has proved to be one of Argentina's most distinctive young voices. His prose has a natural elegance, and his plots display a classical conception of how a novel should be structured . . . *The Oxford Murders* is well crafted and deeply entertaining'

Times Literary Supplement

'It's a tribute to Guillermo Martínez that he has managed to write an intellectual thriller that can be enjoyed even by those – myself included – whose grasp of mathematics is limited'

The Times

'Guillermo Martínez is not only an author but also director of mathematics at the University of Buenos Aires. Like Borges, his writing examines the consequences of abstract theories in the physical world. With a flick of the magician's wrist he questions your ability to explain what is unfolding before your eyes. The shape of the novel is governed as much by the irrationality of people as it is by logical detective work. While creating an atmosphere of suspense, Martínez avoids any formulaic thrills and engages the reader in an enthralling conflict between the heart and the mind'

Observer, Paperback of the Week

'The plot rattles along at an efficient pace, pausing occasionally to fill the reader in with a bit of necessary theoretical background, but never for too long, and always ready with a chilling revelation or another death to get things back up to speed. The narrator and the reader have together been seduced into the thrill of trying to solve an abstract logical puzzle. The unmasking of the culprit reveals that, however much they're dressed up with intellectual fun and games, the motives behind the killings are at once intellectually simpler and emotionally more complex – but not less rational – then was previously supposed'

London Review of Books

'This is a masterpiece of crime writing and a real page-turner with very fascinating, scholarly material for debate. Simply a winner'

New Books Magazine

'Maths and philosophy meet murder in this clever whodunit set in university Oxford. The death of his elderly landlady is the first in a series of murders, linked by cryptic clues and symbols, that will test a visiting Argentinean mathematician, and his friendship with the brilliant logician, Arthur Seldom. Evocative settings and an intriguing, well-constructed plot'

Choice

'Simple storytelling, authentic characters and conceivable situations are brought together in a kind of mathematical-logic whodunit . . . the narrative unfolds in a clever and satisfying way, like a balanced formula'

The List

The Oxford Murders

GUILLERMO MARTÍNEZ

Translated by SONIA SOTO

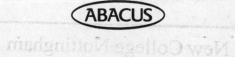

ABACUS

First published in Great Britain in 2005 by Abacus
This edition published in 2008 by Abacus
Reprinted 2008 (twice)

Copyright © Guillermo Martínez 2005
Translation copyright © Sonia Soto 2005

A CIP catalogue record for this book is
available from the British Library.

ISBN 978-0-349-12094-2

Typeset in Sabon by M Rules
Printed and bound in Great Britain by
Clays Ltd, St Ives plc

Papers used by Abacus are natural, renewable and recyclable
products made from wood grown in sustainable forests and certified
in accordance with the rules of the Forest Stewardship Council.

Mixed Sources
Product group from well-managed
forests and other controlled sources
www.fsc.org Cert no. SGS-COC-004081
© 1996 Forest Stewardship Council
FSC

Abacus
An imprint of
Little, Brown Book Group
100 Victoria Embankment
London EC4Y 0DY

An Hachette Livre UK Company
www.hachettelivre.co.uk

www.littlebrown.co.uk

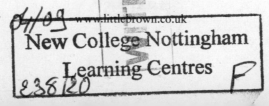

The
Oxford Murders

Chapter 1

Now that the years have passed and everything's been forgotten, and now that I've received a terse e-mail from Scotland with the sad news of Seldom's death, I feel I can break my silence (which he never asked for anyway) and tell the truth about events that reached the British papers in the summer of '93 with macabre and sensationalist headlines, but to which Seldom and I always referred – perhaps due to the mathematical connotation – simply as the series, or the Oxford Series. Indeed, the deaths all occurred in Oxfordshire, at the beginning of my stay in England, and I had the dubious privilege of seeing the first at close range.

I was twenty-two, an age at which almost anything can still be excused. I'd just graduated from the University of Buenos Aires with a thesis in algebraic topology and was travelling to Oxford on a year's scholarship, secretly intending to move over to logic, or at least attend the famous seminars run by Angus MacIntyre. My supervisor, Dr Emily Bronson, had made all the preparations for my arrival with meticulous care. She was a professor and fellow of St Anne's, but in the e-mails we exchanged before my trip she suggested that, instead of staying in the rather uncomfortable college accommodation, I might prefer – grant money allowing – to rent a room with its own bathroom, kitchen and entrance in the house of a Mrs Eagleton, a delightful and discreet lady, she said, the widow of her former professor. I did my sums, as always a little optimistically, and sent off a cheque for advance payment of the first month's rent, the landlady's only requirement.

A fortnight later I was flying over the Atlantic in the incredulous state which overcomes me when I travel: it always seems much more likely, and more economical as a hypothesis – Ockham's Razor, Seldom would have said – that a last-minute accident will send me back to where I started, or to the bottom of the sea, than that an entire country and the immense machinery involved in starting a new life will appear eventually like an outstretched hand down below. And yet, exactly on time, the plane cut calmly through the layer of cloud, and the green hills of England appeared, undeniably true to life, in a light that had suddenly faded, or perhaps I should say deteriorated, because that was my impression: that, as the plane went down, the light was becoming increasingly tenuous, as if it were weakening and languishing, having passed through a filter.

My supervisor had instructed me to take the bus from Heathrow straight to Oxford and apologised several times for not being able to meet me when I arrived as she'd be in London all week at an algebra conference. Far from bothering me, this seemed ideal. I'd have a few days to wander around town and get my bearings, before my academic duties began. I didn't have much luggage, so when the bus arrived at the station I carried my bags across the square to get a taxi. It was the beginning of April but I was glad I'd kept my coat on: there was an icy, cutting wind, and the pallid sun wasn't much help. Even so, I noticed that almost everyone at the fair occupying the square, as well as the Pakistani driver who opened his taxi door for me, was in short sleeves. I gave him Mrs Eagleton's address and as we drove off I asked if he wasn't cold. 'Oh no, it's spring,' he said, waving towards the feeble sun as if this were irrefutable proof.

The black cab advanced sedately towards the main street. As it turned left, I saw, on either side, through half-open wooden gates and iron railings, neat college gardens with immaculate, bright-green lawns. We passed a small graveyard beside a church, with tombstones covered in moss. The taxi went a little way along Banbury Road before turning into Cunliffe Close, the address I had written down. The road now wound through an imposing park. Large, serenely elegant stone houses appeared behind privet hedges, reminding me of Victorian novels with afternoon tea, games of croquet and strolls through the gardens. We checked the house numbers along the road but, judging by the amount of the cheque I'd sent, I couldn't believe that the house I was looking for was one of these. At last, at the end of the road, we came to a row of identical little houses, much more modest but still pleasant, with rectangular wooden balconies and a summery look to them. Mrs Eagleton's was the first house. I unloaded my bags, climbed the small flight of steps at the entrance and rang the bell.

From the dates of her PhD thesis and early published work, I guessed that Emily Bronson must be about fifty-five, so I wondered how old the widow of her former professor might be. The door opened and I saw the angular face and dark-blue eyes of a tall, slim girl not much older than me. She held out her hand, smiling. We stared at each other in pleasant surprise, but then she seemed to draw back cautiously as she freed her hand, which I may have held a little too long. She told me her name, Beth, and tried to repeat mine, not entirely successfully, before showing me into a very cosy sitting room with a rug patterned with red and grey lozenges.

Mrs Eagleton sat in a floral armchair and held out her hand, smiling welcomingly. The old lady had twinkling eyes and a lively manner, and her white hair was carefully arranged in a bun. As I crossed the room, I noticed that there was a wheelchair folded up and leaning against the back of her armchair. A tartan blanket was laid over her legs. We shook hands and I felt her frail, slightly tremulous fingers. She held my hand warmly for a moment, patting it with her other hand, and asked about my journey and whether this was my first visit to England.

'We weren't expecting someone so young, were we, Beth?' she said with surprise.

Beth, standing by the door, smiled but said nothing. She took a key from a hook on the wall and, after I'd answered a few more questions, she suggested gently:

4

'Don't you think, grandmother, that we should show him to his room now? He must be terribly tired.'

'Of course,' said Mrs Eagleton. 'Beth will explain everything. And if you don't have anything else planned this evening, we'd be delighted if you'd join us for dinner.'

I followed Beth out of the house and down a little flight of steps to the basement. She stooped slightly as she opened the small front door and showed me into a large, tidy room. Though below ground level, it received quite a lot of light from two windows, very high up by the ceiling. Beth began explaining all the little details as she walked about the room, opening drawers and showing me cupboards, cutlery and towels, in a kind of recitation that she must have repeated many times. I checked out the bed and the shower, but mainly I looked at her. Her skin was dry, tanned, taut, as if she spent a lot of time outdoors, and although it made her look healthy, it also made her look in danger of ageing early.

At first I'd thought she was in her early twenties but now, seeing her in different light, I realised that she must be nearer twenty-seven or twenty-eight. Her eyes were particularly intriguing: they were a very beautiful deep blue, but they seemed more still than the rest of her features, as if reluctant to express emotion. She was wearing a long, loose peasant dress with a round neck, which didn't give much away about her body other than that she was thin, although looking more closely I saw hints that, luckily, she wasn't thin all over. From the back, especially, she looked very huggable. Like all tall girls, there was something slightly vulnerable about her. When our eyes met again she asked me – without irony, I think – if there was

5

anything else I wanted to check out. I looked away, embarrassed, and quickly answered that everything seemed fine. Before she left I asked, taking much too long to get to the point, whether I really should consider myself invited to dinner. She laughed and said that of course I should, and that they'd expect me at six-thirty.

I unpacked my few belongings, piled some books and copies of my thesis on the desk and put my clothes away in the drawers. After that I went for a walk around town. At one end of St Giles, I spotted the Mathematical Institute straight away: it was the only hideous modern building. I looked at the front steps and the revolving door at the entrance, and decided that I could give it a miss on my first day. I bought a sandwich and had a solitary and rather late picnic lunch on the banks of the river, watching a rowing team train. I browsed in a few bookshops, stopped to admire the gargoyles on the cornices of a theatre, followed a tour group around the courtyards of one of the colleges and then went for a long walk through the University Parks. In an area edged by trees a man on a machine was mowing large rectangular sections of grass and another man was marking out the lines of a tennis court. I stood and watched nostalgically. When they stopped for a break I asked when the nets would be going up. I'd given up tennis in my second year at university and hadn't brought my rackets with me, but I promised myself I'd buy a new one and find a partner.

On the way back I went into a supermarket for a few supplies and then took time finding an off-licence, where I chose a bottle of wine for dinner more or less at random.

When I got back to Cunliffe Close, it was only just after six but it was already dark and there were lights on in all the houses. I was surprised to see that nobody drew their curtains; I wondered if this was due to (possibly excessive) faith in the spirit of discretion of the English, who wouldn't stoop to spying on the life of others; or perhaps to an equally English certainty that they wouldn't do anything in private that was worth spying on. There weren't any shutters anywhere and I had the feeling that most doors weren't locked.

I had a shower, shaved, selected my least crumpled shirt and, at exactly six-thirty, went up the little flight of steps and rang the bell, carrying my bottle. The dinner passed in an atmosphere of polite, smiling, rather bland cordiality which I'd get used to in time. Beth had smartened herself up a little, though she still wasn't wearing make-up. She had changed into a black silk blouse and brushed her hair so that it fell seductively over one side of her face. But none of it was for me: I soon found out that she played the cello with the chamber orchestra of the Sheldonian Theatre, the semicircular building with the gargoyles that I'd seen on my walk. They were having their final rehearsal that evening and some lucky man called Michael was picking her up in half an hour. There was a brief, awkward silence when, assuming that he must be, I asked if he was her boyfriend. The two women exchanged glances but as my only answer Mrs Eagleton asked if I'd like more potato salad. For the rest of the meal Beth seemed slightly absent and in the end the conversation was entirely between me and Mrs Eagleton.

The doorbell rang and, after Beth left, my hostess

became noticeably more animated, as if an invisible thread of tension had slackened. She poured herself a second glass of wine and for a long time I listened to her talk about her eventful, remarkable life. During the war she'd been one of a small number of women who entered a national crossword competition, in all innocence, only to find that the prize was to be recruited and confined to an isolated little village, with the mission of helping Alan Turing and his team of mathematicians decipher the codes of the Nazis' Enigma machine. That was where she met Mr Eagleton. She recounted lots of anecdotes about the war and also the circumstances surrounding Turing's famous poisoning.

When she moved to Oxford, she said, she gave up crosswords and took up Scrabble instead, which she played with a group of friends whenever she could. She wheeled herself briskly over to a little low table in the sitting room, and told me to follow her and not to worry about clearing the table, Beth would take care of it when she got back. I watched apprehensively as she took a Scrabble board from a drawer and unfolded it. I couldn't refuse. So that's how I spent the rest of my first evening in Oxford: trying to form words in English, sitting opposite an almost historical old lady who, every two or three goes, used up all her seven letters, laughing like a little girl.

Chapter 2

I went to the Mathematical Institute a couple of days later and was given a desk in the visitors' office, an e-mail account and a swipe card for getting into the library out of hours. There was only one other occupant of the office, a Russian called Podorov, and we exchanged brief greetings. He paced up and down the room, slouching, and occasionally leaned over his desk to scribble a formula in a large hardback notebook that looked like a book of psalms. Every half hour he went out and smoked a cigarette in the little paved courtyard outside the window.

Early the following week I had my first meeting with Emily Bronson, a tiny woman with very straight white hair, held back with hair clips like a schoolgirl's. She rode to the Institute on a bicycle that was too big for her, with a basket for her books and packed lunch. She looked a little like a nun, and seemed shy, but in time I found that she had a razor-sharp sense of humour. Despite her modesty I think she was flattered that I had called my thesis 'Bronson's Spaces'. At our first meeting she gave me copies of her last two papers, and a handful of brochures and maps of places to visit in Oxford before, she said, the new term began and I had less free time. She asked if there was anything in particular I missed about life in Buenos Aires and when I hinted that I'd like to take up tennis again she assured me, with a smile that showed she was accustomed to far more eccentric requests, that it would be easy to arrange.

Two days later I found an invitation in my pigeonhole to play doubles at a tennis club in Marston Ferry Road, a few minutes' walk from Cunliffe Close. The group was made up of John, an American photographer with long arms who was good at the net; Sammy, a Canadian biologist who was almost an albino, energetic and tireless; and Lorna, a nurse at the Radcliffe Hospital, of Irish extraction, with flaming red hair and sparkling, seductive green eyes.

To the pleasure of stepping back on to a tennis court was added a second, unexpected pleasure of finding, at the other end of the court, during our initial knock-up, a woman who was not only fascinating but who had confident, elegant ground strokes and returned all my shots low over the net. We played three sets, changing partners. Lorna and I made a smiling and fearsome duo, and I spent the following week counting the days until I was back on the court and then the games until she was playing by my side again.

I bumped into Mrs Eagleton almost every morning. Sometimes I found her gardening, very early, as I was leaving for the Mathematical Institute, and we'd exchange a few words. Or I'd see her on Banbury Road, heading to the shops in her electric wheelchair, when I was taking a break to buy lunch. She glided serenely along the pavement as if on a boat, bowing her head graciously to students as they moved out of her way. By contrast, I very rarely saw Beth. I'd only spoken to her again once, one afternoon as I was arriving back from tennis. Lorna had given me a lift to Cunliffe Close in her car and, as I was saying goodbye, I saw Beth getting off a bus with her cello. I went to help her carry it into the house. It was one of the first really warm days and I suppose I must have looked tanned after an afternoon in the sun. She smiled accusingly at me.

'Well, I see you've settled in. Shouldn't you be studying maths instead of playing tennis and riding around in cars with women?'

'I've got permission from my director of studies,' I said, laughing, and made a sign of absolution.

'Oh, I'm just teasing. Actually, I envy you.'

'Envy me? Why?'

'Oh, I don't know. You seem so free. You've left your country, your other life, everything behind. And a fortnight later, here you are, happy and tanned and playing tennis.'

'You should try it. You just have to apply for a grant.'

She shook her head sadly.

'I've tried, I've already tried, but it seems it's too late. They'd never admit it, of course, but they prefer to give

11

them to younger women. I'm almost twenty-nine,' she said, as if that were the start of old age. She added, bitterly: 'Sometimes I'd give anything to get away from here.'

I gazed at the ivy-clad houses, the spires on top of medieval cupolas, the crenellated towers in the distance.

'Get away from Oxford? I can't imagine a more beautiful place.'

A look of futility dulled her eyes.

'Yes, maybe . . . if you didn't have to look after an invalid all the time and spend your days doing something that lost all meaning long ago.'

'Don't you like playing the cello?' I found this surprising, and interesting. I looked at her, trying to see what lay beneath the surface.

'I hate it,' she said, and her eyes grew dark. 'I hate it more every day, and it's getting harder and harder to hide. Sometimes I'm scared that it shows when I play, that the conductor or one of my colleagues will realise how much I detest each note. But at the end of every concert the audience claps and nobody seems to notice anything. Isn't that funny?'

'I'd say you're safe. I don't think hatred has its own special vibration. In that sense, music is as abstract as maths: it doesn't make moral distinctions. As long as you follow the score, I don't imagine there's any way of detecting it.'

'Follow the score . . . that's what I've done all my life,' she sighed. We were at the front door now and she put her hand on the doorknob. 'Don't take any notice of me,' she said, 'I've had a bad day.'

'But the day isn't over yet,' I said. 'Is there anything I can do to improve it?'

12

She smiled sadly and took the cello from me.

'Oh, you're such a Latin man,' she murmured, as if that were something she should be wary of. Still, before she shut the door, she allowed me a last glimpse of her blue eyes.

Two weeks passed. Summer was slowly starting, with mild evenings and very long sunsets. On the first Wednesday in May, on my way home from the Institute, I stopped at a cash machine to get money for my rent. I rang Mrs Eagleton's doorbell and, as I waited, a man came up the winding path to the house. He was tall and took large strides, and he looked preoccupied. I peered at him out of the corner of my eye as he came to a stop beside me. He had a wide, high forehead and small, deep-set eyes, and a noticeable scar on his chin. He must have been in his mid-fifties, but a kind of contained energy in his move-ments made him seem still young. There was a brief moment of awkwardness as we both waited at the closed door, until he asked, in a deep, melodious Scottish accent, if I had rung the bell. I said I had and rang for a second time. I said perhaps my first ring had been too brief. As I spoke the man gave me a friendly smile and asked if I was Argentinian.

'So you must be Emily's graduate student,' he said, switching to perfect Spanish with – amusingly – a Buenos Aires accent.

Surprised, I said that I was and asked him where he had learned Spanish. He arched his eyebrows, as if looking into the distant past, and said he'd learned it many years ago.

'My first wife was from Buenos Aires.' He held out his hand. 'I'm Arthur Seldom.'

At that time few names could have provoked more admiration in me. The man with the small, pale eyes holding out his hand was already a legend among mathematicians. I'd spent months studying his most famous work, the philosophical extension of Gödel's theorem from the thirties, for a seminar. He was considered one of the four leading minds in the field of logic, and you just had to glance at the varied titles of his work to see that he was a rare case of mathematical genius. Beneath that high, serene forehead some of the most profound ideas of the century had fallen into place. On my second visit to the bookshops in town I had tried to get hold of his latest book, a popular work explaining logical series, and found, to my surprise, that it had been sold out for a couple of months. Someone mentioned that, since the book's publication, Seldom had disappeared from the conference circuit and apparently nobody dared venture a guess as to what he was working on now. In any case I didn't even know he lived in Oxford, and I certainly never would have expected to bump into him at Mrs Eagleton's front door. I told him I'd expounded on his theorem at a seminar and he seemed pleased by my enthusiasm. But he was obviously worried about something as he kept glancing at the door.

'Mrs Eagleton should be in, shouldn't she?' he said.

'I would have thought so,' I said. 'There's her electric wheelchair. Unless someone's taken her out by car.'

Seldom rang the bell again and listened at the door. He went to the window that looked on to the hall, and peered inside.

14

'Is there a back door?' And then, in English, he said: 'I'm worried something might have happened to her.'

I could tell from his face that he was deeply alarmed, as if he knew something that stopped him concentrating on anything else.

'We could try the door,' I said. 'I don't think they lock it during the day.'

Seldom turned the handle and the door opened quietly. We entered without a word, the wooden floorboards creaking beneath our steps. Inside we could hear, like a muffled heartbeat, the stealthy to and fro of a clock's pendulum. We went through to the sitting room and stopped by the table in the centre. I pointed to the chaise longue by the window looking on to the garden. Mrs Eagleton was lying there, apparently sleeping deeply, her face turned towards the back of the chair. One of her pillows was on the floor, as if it had slipped while she slept. Her bun of white hair was carefully protected by a hairnet and her glasses lay on the little table, beside the Scrabble board. It looked as if she had been playing on her own because the letter racks were both on her side.

Seldom went over to her. As he touched her lightly on the shoulder her head fell heavily to one side. Just then we saw her terrified open eyes and two parallel trails of blood running from her nose to her chin, joining on her neck. Involuntarily I took a step back and had to stop myself from crying out. Seldom, who was supporting her head with his arm, rearranged the body as best he could and muttered something anxiously that I didn't catch. He picked up the pillow, uncovering a big red stain on the carpet that was almost dry in the centre. He stood for a moment with his arm down by his side, holding the pillow, deep in thought, as if exploring the ramifications of a complex calculation. He looked truly perturbed. I said I thought we ought to call the police and he agreed mechanically.

Chapter 3

'They said we should wait outside,' said Seldom laconi-
cally when he hung up.

We went out to the little porch, making sure not to
touch anything. Seldom leaned against the handrail and
rolled a cigarette. His hands paused from time to time as
he folded the cigarette paper, then compulsively repeated
an action, as if they were following the stops and starts of
a train of thought that he had to check carefully. He no
longer looked overwhelmed, as he had a few moments
earlier; instead he seemed to be trying to make sense of
something incomprehensible.

Two policemen arrived and stationed themselves silently
in front of the house. A tall, grey-haired man with piercing
eyes, wearing a dark-blue suit, came up to us. He shook
hands with us quickly and asked for our names. He had
prominent cheekbones, probably growing sharper with

age, and a look of calm but determined authority, as if he was used to taking charge of situations.

'I'm Inspector Petersen,' he said. He indicated a man in green overalls who nodded briefly as he came past. 'That's our forensic pathologist. Would you mind coming inside for a moment? We need to ask you some questions.'

The pathologist put on latex gloves and leaned over the chaise longue. We watched from across the room as he carefully checked Mrs Eagleton's body, taking blood and skin samples, which he handed to one of his assistants. The photographer's flash went off a couple of times above the lifeless face.

'Right,' said the pathologist, beckoning to us. 'In exactly what position did you find her?'

'Her head was facing the back of the sofa,' said Seldom. 'She was on her side . . . a little bit more . . . Her legs were straight, the right arm was bent. Yes, I think she was like that.' He glanced at me for confirmation.

'And that pillow was on the floor,' I added.

Petersen picked up the pillow and showed the forensic pathologist the bloodstain in the middle.

'Do you remember exactly where?'

'On the rug, about level with her head. It looked as if it fell while she was asleep.'

The photographer took another couple of photos.

'I believe,' the pathologist said to Petersen, 'that whoever did this meant to smother her without leaving any trace, while she was sleeping. He took the pillow from under her head very carefully, without disarranging the hairnet, or perhaps he found the pillow already on the floor. But while he was pressing it over her face, she woke

18

up and maybe put up a fight. And this is when our man got scared, pressed down with the back of his hand or possibly even pushed with his knee to get more pressure, and crushed her nose under the pillow without realising. That's all it is: a little blood from the nose. At that age the blood vessels are very fragile. When he removed the pillow he found the face all covered in blood. He may have got scared again and dropped the pillow on the floor without trying to put things back as they were. Maybe he decided that it didn't matter and just got out as quickly as he could. I think this is someone who's killing for the first time. Probably right-handed.' He held his arms above Mrs Eagleton's face to demonstrate. 'Judging by where the pillow ended up on the carpet, I'd say he turned like this. That would be the most natural movement for a person holding it with their right hand.'

'Male or female?' asked Petersen.

'Now that's interesting,' said the pathologist. 'It could have been a strong man who damaged her by simply pressing down harder with the palm of his hand, or a woman who felt too weak and maintained the pressure by pushing down with the full weight of her body.'

'Time of death?'

'Between two and three in the afternoon.' The forensic pathologist then turned to us. 'What time did you get here?'

'It was four-thirty,' Seldom said, looking at me quickly for confirmation. And then, addressing Petersen: 'I think she was probably killed at three.'

The inspector looked at him with a spark of interest.

'Really? How do you know?'

'We didn't arrive together,' said Seldom. 'I came because of a note, a rather strange message I found in my pigeon-hole at Merton. Unfortunately, I didn't pay much attention to it at first. But I expect it would have been too late anyway.'

'What was the message?'

'"The first of the series",' said Seldom. 'That's all. In large, handwritten capitals. And underneath, Mrs Eagleton's address and the time, as if it were an appointment: 3 p.m.'

'Could I see it? Did you bring it with you?'

Seldom shook his head.

'When I collected it from my pigeonhole it was already gone three and I was late for my seminar. I read it on the way to my office and, frankly, I thought it must be yet another message from a madman. My book on logical series came out recently and I foolishly included a chapter on serial killers. Since then I've received all kinds of letters confessing to murders . . . Anyway, I threw the note in the wastepaper basket as soon as I got back to my office.'

'In that case, might it still be there?' asked Petersen.

'I'm afraid not,' said Seldom. 'When I came out of my class I remembered the note. The Cunliffe Close address had left me a little anxious: during the class I remembered that that was where Mrs Eagleton lived, though I wasn't sure of the house number. I thought I'd better reread the note, to confirm the address, but the porter had been in to clean my office and had emptied the wastepaper basket. That's why I decided to come here.'

'We could try to find it anyway,' said Petersen, and he called over one of his men. 'Wilkie, could you go to

Merton College and have a word with the porter? What's the man's name?'

'Brent,' said Seldom. 'But I don't think it'll be any use. The refuse lorry must have been by now.'

'If it doesn't turn up we'll call you so you can give our police artist a description of the handwriting. We're going to keep this to ourselves for now, so I'd ask you both for your utmost discretion. Can you remember anything else about the note? The type of paper, ink colour, or anything that drew your attention.'

'It was in black ink, from a fountain pen, I think. The paper was ordinary white notepaper. The handwriting was large and clear. The note was carefully folded in four in my pigeonhole. And yes, there was something intriguing: under the words there was a neatly drawn circle. A small perfect circle, also in black.'

'A circle,' repeated Petersen thoughtfully. 'Like a signature? A stamp? Or does it mean something else to you?'

'It may have something to do with the chapter on serial murders in my book,' said Seldom. 'In it I maintain that, except in crime novels and films, the logic behind serial murders – at least those that have been documented historically – is generally very rudimentary, and relates to pathological mental states. The patterns are very crude, typified by monotony, repetition, and the overwhelming majority are based on some traumatic experience or childhood fixation. In other words, they're cases that should be subjected to psychoanalysis rather than being true logical enigmas. In the chapter I conclude that crimes motivated by intellectual concerns, by intellectual vanity, like Raskolnikov's or, in its artistic

21

variant, Thomas de Quincey's, would seem not to belong to the real world. Or else, as I suggest playfully in the book, the perpetrators were so clever that they were never found out.'

'I see,' said Petersen. 'You think that someone who read your book took up the challenge. So in that case the circle would be . . .'

'Possibly the first symbol in a logical series,' said Seldom. 'It would be a good choice: it's a symbol that historically has probably had the greatest variety of interpretations, both in the world of mathematics and outside. It can mean almost anything. It's a clever way to start a series: putting the symbol of maximum uncertainty at the beginning, so that we're almost totally in the dark as to how it might continue.'

'Do you think this person is a mathematician?'

'No, not necessarily. My publishers were surprised at what a varied audience my book reached. And we still don't even know whether we should interpret the symbol as a circle. I mean, the first thing I saw was a circle, possibly because of my mathematical training. But it could be a symbol from some esoteric cult, or ancient religion, or something else entirely. An astrologer might have seen a full moon, or your artist might have seen the outline of a face . . .'

'All right,' said Petersen, 'let's go back to Mrs Eagleton for a moment. Did you know her well?'

'Harry Eagleton was my tutor and they invited me to some of their parties and to dinner here after I graduated. And I was friends with their son, Johnny, and his wife, Sarah. They were both killed in an accident, when Beth was a child. She's lived with Mrs Eagleton ever since. I haven't seen much of them lately. I knew that Mrs Eagleton had been suffering from cancer for some time, and that she'd had to go into hospital on several occasions. I saw her at the Radcliffe a couple of times.'

'And this girl, Beth, does she still live here? How old is she now?'

'She must be about twenty-nine, thirty. And yes, she lives with Mrs Eagleton.'

'We need to see her as soon as possible. I need to ask her a few questions too,' said Petersen. 'Does either of you know where I might find her?'

'She must be at the Sheldonian,' I said. 'Rehearsing.'

'I pass the theatre on my way home,' said Seldom. 'If you don't mind, I'd like to request that you let me, as a friend of the family, break the news to her. She might also need help with the funeral arrangements.'

'Of course, that's fine,' said Petersen. 'But the funeral will have to wait: we've got to get a post-mortem done first. Please tell Beth that we'll wait for her here. The fingerprints people still have work to do, we'll probably be here another couple of hours. It was you who phoned the police, wasn't it? Do you remember if either of you touched anything else?'

We shook our heads. Petersen called one of his men, who came carrying a small tape recorder.

'In that case I'll just ask you to give a brief statement to Detective Sergeant Sacks about your movements from midday today. It's routine. After that you're free to go, though I'm afraid I may have to bother you both with more questions over the next few days.'

Seldom spent two or three minutes answering the detective's questions. When it was my turn I noticed that he stood discreetly to one side waiting for me to finish. I thought he might have wanted to say goodbye, but when I turned to him he indicated that we should leave together.

Chapter 4

'I thought we might walk to the Sheldonian together,' said Seldom, rolling another cigarette. 'I'd like to know . . .' He hesitated, struggling for the right words. It was now completely dark outside, so I couldn't see his face. 'I'd like to be sure,' he said at last, 'that we both saw the same thing in there. I mean, before the police arrived, before all the theories and explanations – the original scene as we found it. I'd like to know your first impression as, of the two of us, you'd had no warning.'

I thought for a moment, trying to remember, to reconstruct the exact scene. I was aware too that I wanted to appear sharp and not disappoint Seldom.

'I think,' I said, 'I agree with almost everything the pathologist said, except maybe for one final detail. He thought that when the murderer saw the blood, he dropped the pillow and got out as quickly as possible, without trying to put things back.'

'But you don't think that's what happened?'

'He may not have tried to tidy up, but he did do one more thing before leaving: he turned Mrs Eagleton's face towards the back of the chaise longue. That's how we found her.'

'You're right,' said Seldom, nodding slowly. 'What do you think it means?'

'I don't know, maybe he couldn't bear to see Mrs Eagleton's staring eyes. If, as the pathologist said, this was someone who was killing for the first time, he may have seen her eyes, suddenly realised what he'd done and tried to put them out of his sight somehow.'

'Do you think he knew Mrs Eagleton, or did he pick her more or less at random?'

'I don't think it was totally random. What you said afterwards drew my attention – that Mrs Eagleton had cancer. Perhaps he knew that she was going to die soon anyway. That would seem to fit with the idea of a challenge that's mainly intellectual, as if he wanted to do as little damage as possible. If it hadn't been for her waking up, even the method he chose to kill her could have been seen as fairly merciful. Perhaps what he knew,' it occurred to me suddenly, 'was that *you* knew Mrs Eagleton and that it would force you to get involved.'

'That's possible,' said Seldom. 'And I agree that he wanted to kill in the most subtle way possible. What I was wondering while we were listening to the pathologist was what would have happened if things had gone according to plan and Mrs Eagleton's nose hadn't bled.'

'Only you would have known – thanks to the note – that she hadn't died of natural causes.'

'Exactly,' said Seldom. 'In principle the police wouldn't have been involved. I think that was what he wanted – a private challenge.'

'Yes, but in that case,' I said, doubtful, 'I don't understand when he wrote the note – before or after killing her.'

'Perhaps he wrote it before killing her,' said Seldom, 'and even when part of the plan went awry, he decided to carry on and leave it in my pigeonhole anyway.'

'What do you think he'll do now?'

'Now that the police have been informed? I don't know. I suppose he'll try to be more careful next time.'

'You mean, another murder that no one will see as a murder?'

'That's right,' said Seldom, almost to himself. 'Exactly. Murders that no one sees as murders. I think I'm starting to see now: imperceptible murders.'

We were silent for a moment. Seldom was deep in thought. We were almost at the University Parks. Across the road, a large limousine drew up outside a restaurant. A bride emerged, dragging her heavy train and holding on to the pretty headdress of flowers in her hair. A small group of people crowded round her and cameras flashed. Seldom didn't seem to notice any of it: he walked staring straight ahead, utterly absorbed in his own thoughts. Even so, I decided to interrupt him and ask about the point that was most intriguing me.

'Regarding what you said to the inspector, about the circle and the logical series, don't you think there must be

27

a connection between the symbol and the choice of victim, or perhaps with the method he chose to kill her?'

'Yes, probably,' said Seldom, slightly absent-mindedly, as if he'd already gone over this much earlier. 'But as I told Petersen, the thing is, we can't even be sure if it is a circle or, to pick an example at random, the Gnostics' ouroboros – the serpent biting its own tail – or the O from the word "omertà". That's the problem when you know only the first term of a series: establishing the context in which the symbol is to be read. I mean, whether you should consider it from a purely graphic point of view, for instance, on a syntactic level, simply as a figure, or on a semantic level, due to one of the possible meanings attributed to it. There's a fairly well-known series that I use as a first example at the start of my book to explain this ambiguity. Now let me see . . .'

He searched his pockets until he found a pencil and a little notebook, then tore out a page and rested it on the cover of the notebook. Still walking, he carefully drew three figures and handed me the paper. We'd reached Magdalen Street, so I could make them out easily by the light of the street lights. The first figure was definitely a capital M, the second looked like a heart above a line and the third was the number 8:

M ♡ 8

'What do you think the fourth figure is?' Seldom asked.

'M, heart, eight . . .' I said, trying to make sense of them. Seldom waited, a little amused, while I pondered.

'I'm sure you'll find the answer if you give it some

thought quietly at home this evening,' he said. 'I simply wanted to show you that, at this stage, it's as if we'd been given only the first symbol in a series,' he said and covered the heart and the eight with his hand. 'If you saw only this figure – the letter M – what would you think?'

'That it's a series of letters, or the beginning of a word that starts with M.'

'Exactly,' said Seldom. 'You would have given the symbol the meaning not just of a letter in general, but of a precise, specific letter, a capital M. But as soon as you see the second symbol of the series, things look different, don't they? You now know that you can no longer expect a word, for instance. The second symbol is quite unlike the first, quite different. It might remind you of playing cards, for instance. Anyway, to a certain extent, it puts in doubt the initial meaning we gave to the first symbol. We can still think of it as a letter, but it no longer seems so important that it's specifically an m. And when we bring in the third symbol, again, our first instinct is to reorder it all in accordance with what we know: if we interpret it as the number eight, we're thinking of a series that begins with a letter, continues with a heart, continues with a number. But note that we're pondering all the time meanings that we're assigning, almost automatically, to what are in principle merely drawings, lines on a piece of paper. That's what's so cunning about the series: it's difficult to separate the three figures from their most obvious, immediate interpretation. Now, if for a moment you can see the naked symbols simply as figures, you'll find the constant that eradicates all previous meanings and gives you the key to how the series continues.'

We passed the brightly lit windows of the Eagle and

Child. Inside, people were standing at the bar, laughing soundlessly as they raised their pints of beer, as if they were in a silent film. We crossed the road and turned left, skirting around a monument. The curved wall of the theatre appeared in front of us.

'You mean that in this case, in order to establish the context, we need at least one more term.'

'Yes,' said Seldom. 'With only the first symbol we're still completely in the dark. We can't even determine which direction to take first: whether we should consider the symbol simply as a mark on a paper, or try to attribute some meaning to it. Unfortunately, all we can do is wait.'

He climbed the steps to the theatre as he spoke and I followed, reluctant to let him go. The foyer was deserted but we were guided by the sound of the music, which was light and joyful like a dance. Trying to be as quiet as possible, we went upstairs and along a carpeted corridor. Seldom opened one of the doors leading off it, which had diamond-shaped padding, and we entered a box with a view of the small orchestra on stage. It was rehearsing what sounded like a Hungarian csárdás. We could now hear the music clearly and loudly.

Beth was leaning forward in her chair, her body tense, her bow moving backwards and forwards furiously across the cello. I listened to the dizzying rush of notes, like whips lashing against horses' flanks, and in the contrast between the lightness and joyfulness of the music and the efforts of the players I remembered what Beth had told me a few days earlier. Her face was transformed as she concentrated on the music. Her fingers moved quickly over the fingerboard but there was something distant in her eyes, as if only part of her were there. Seldom and I went back out into the corridor. He looked grave, reserved, but I realised he was nervous because he started rolling another cigarette mechanically, even though he wouldn't be able to smoke there. I said goodbye and Seldom shook my hard firmly. He thanked me again for having accompanied him.

'If you're free on Friday,' he said, 'would you like to have lunch with me at Merton? Perhaps we can come up with something else between now and then.'

'I'd love to. Friday would be perfect for me,' I said.

I went down the stairs and back out to the street. It was cold now and drizzling. Standing under a street light, I took out the piece of paper on which Seldom had drawn the three figures, trying to shield it from the fine rain. I almost laughed out loud when, halfway home, I realised how simple the answer was.

Chapter 5

As I rounded the last bend of the close and came up to the house I saw that the police were still there. An ambulance was there now too and a blue van with the logo of the *Oxford Times*. A lanky man with curly grey hair flopping over his forehead stopped me on my way down to my room. He was holding a small tape recorder and a notebook. Before he could introduce himself, Inspector Petersen leaned out of the hall window and asked me to come upstairs.

'I'd rather you didn't mention this to anyone,' he said quietly. 'We gave your name only to the press, as if you were on your own when you found the body.'

I nodded and went back to the top of the steps. While I was answering the reporter's questions I saw a taxi draw up. Beth got out with her cello and went past without seeing us. She had to give her name to the policeman at the door before she was allowed inside. Her voice sounded weak and slightly strangled.

'So that's the girl,' said the reporter glancing at his watch. 'I need to talk to her too. Looks like I'm going to miss my supper. One last thing: what did Petersen just say to you, when he called you over?'

I hesitated a moment.

'That they might have to bother me with more questions tomorrow,' I said.

'Don't worry,' he said, 'you're not a suspect.'

I laughed.

'So who is?' I asked.

'I don't know, the girl, I suppose. It's what you'd expect, isn't it? She's the one who's going to end up with the money and the house.'

'I didn't know Mrs Eagleton had money.'

'War Heroes' Pension. It's not a fortune, but for a woman on her own . . .'

'But wasn't Beth already in rehearsal at the time of the murder?'

The man flicked back through his notebook.

'Let's see: according to the pathologist's report, time of death was between two and three. One of the neighbours saw the girl leave for the Sheldonian a little after two. I called the theatre just now: she got to the rehearsal at exactly two-thirty. But that still leaves a few minutes, before she left. Which means she was in the house, she could have done it, and she's the only beneficiary.'

'Are you going to put that in your article?' I asked. I think I sounded a little indignant.

'Why not? It's more interesting than blaming it on a

burglar and telling housewives to keep their doors locked. I'm going to try to have a word with her now.' He smiled mischievously. 'Read my article tomorrow.'

I went down to my room and, without turning on the light, took my shoes off and lay down on the bed, one arm over my eyes. I tried again to reconstruct in memory the moment when Seldom and I entered the house and the sequence of our movements, but I couldn't find anything else there, at least not the kind of thing Seldom was looking for. All that reappeared vividly in my mind was the disjointed movement of Mrs Eagleton's neck as her head fell to one side, eyes wide open and terrified. A car engine started up and I raised myself on my elbows to look out of the window. I saw them bring Mrs Eagleton's corpse out on a stretcher and load it into the ambulance. The police cars switched on their headlights and, as they turned around, yellow cones of light created a succession of fleeting, phantasmagorical shadows on the walls of the houses. The *Oxford Times* van had already left and once the small convoy of vehicles had disappeared around the first bend, I found the silence and darkness of the close oppressive for the first time. I wondered what Beth was doing upstairs, alone in the house. I switched on the light and saw Emily Bronson's papers, with my notes in the margins, on the desk. I made coffee and sat down, intending to continue where I'd left off. I worked for over an hour, but didn't get much further. Nor did I attain that merciful calm, that singular mental balm – apparent order within chaos – that comes as you follow the steps of a theorem.

Suddenly I thought I heard gentle knocking at the door. I pushed the chair back and waited a moment. I heard the knocking again, more clearly this time. I opened the door and in the darkness made out Beth's slightly embarrassed face. She was wearing a lilac dressing gown and slippers, and her hair was simply held back by a hairband, as if she had rushed from her bed. I told her to come in. She stood just inside the door, arms crossed, lips trembling slightly.

'Could I ask you a favour? Just for tonight,' she said in a faltering voice. 'I can't get to sleep up there. Can I stay here till morning?'

'Of course you can,' I said. 'I'll make up the sofa, and you can have the bed.'

She thanked me, relieved, and collapsed on to one of the chairs. She looked around, dazed, and saw my papers spread out over the desk.

'You were working,' she said. 'I don't want to disturb you.'

'No, no,' I said, 'I was about to take a break anyway. I couldn't concentrate. Shall I make coffee?'

'I'd rather have tea, if that's OK,' she said.

We remained silent while I put the kettle on and searched for a suitable phrase of condolence. But she spoke first.

'Uncle Arthur told me you were with him when he found her. It must have been awful. I had to see her too: they made me identify the body. God,' she said, and her eyes turned watery, a liquid, trembling blue, 'nobody had bothered to close her eyes.'

She looked away, tilting her head slightly, trying to hold back the tears.

'I'm so sorry,' I murmured. 'I know how you must be feeling.'

35

'No, I don't think you do,' she said. 'I don't think anyone can. It was what I'd been hoping for for a long time. For years. Though it may be terrible to say so, ever since I found out she had cancer. I'd always imagined it would happen almost exactly as it did – that someone would come to tell me, in the middle of a rehearsal. I prayed that it would be like that, that I wouldn't have to see her before they took her away. But the inspector wanted me to identify her. They hadn't closed her eyes!' she said again in an anxious whisper, as if this were an inexplicable injustice. 'I stood there but I couldn't look at her; I was afraid that she could still somehow hurt me, drag me with her, not let go. And I think she's succeeded: I'm a suspect,' she said dejectedly. 'Petersen asked me lots of questions, with that mock-considerate manner of his. And then that horrible man from the paper, he didn't even try to hide it. I told them all I know: that when I left at two she was asleep, next to the Scrabble table. But I don't feel I've got the strength to defend myself. I'm the person who most wanted to see her dead, much more, I'm sure, than whoever killed her.'

She seemed to be consumed by nervousness, her hands shaking uncontrollably. When she caught my look she crossed her arms.

'Anyway,' I said, handing her a cup of tea, 'I don't think Petersen is thinking any of this: they know something which they don't want to make public. Didn't Professor Seldom say anything?'

She shook her head and I was sorry I had spoken. But I saw the expectant look in her blue eyes, as if she scarcely dared hope, and decided that Latin indiscretion could be kinder than English reserve.

'This is all I can tell you, because they asked us to keep it secret. The person who killed your grandmother left Seldom a message in his pigeonhole. In the note there was your address and a time, three in the afternoon.'

'Three in the afternoon,' she repeated slowly. A huge weight seemed to be lifting from her. 'I was in rehearsal by then.' She smiled weakly, as if a long, difficult battle were over. She took a sip of tea and looked at me gratefully over the cup.

'Beth,' I started. Her hand lay in her lap quite close to mine and I had to stop myself touching it. 'About what you said before – if I can help in any way with the funeral arrangements, or anything else, please ask. I'm sure Professor Seldom, or Michael, must have offered already . . .'

'Michael?' she said, and laughed drily. 'He won't be much help, this whole business terrifies him.' And she added rather contemptuously, as if referring to a particularly cowardly species: 'He's a married man.'

She stood up and, before I could stop her, went over to the sink beside the desk and washed her cup.

'Uncle Arthur's a mathematical genius, isn't he?' Beth said proudly.

'One of the greatest,' I said.

She took off her hairband, placing it on the bedside table, and shook out her hair. Then she went over to the bed and pulled back the eiderdown. Her hand went to the neck of her dressing gown.

'Do you mind turning around for a moment,' she said, 'I'd like to take this off.'

I carried my own cup to the sink. After turning off the

tap, I stood with my back to her a moment longer. She said my name, making an endearing effort to pronounce it correctly. She was in bed, her hair spread seductively over the pillow. She had pulled the eiderdown almost up to her chin but one arm lay outside.

'Could I ask you one last favour? It's something my mother used to do when I was little. Could you hold my hand until I fall asleep?'

'Of course,' I said. I turned off the light and sat down on the edge of the bed. Moonlight seeped weakly through the window, lighting up her bare arm. I placed my palm on top of hers and we interlaced our fingers at the same time. Her hand was warm and dry. I looked more closely at the soft skin on the back of her hand and her long fingers, with their short, neat nails, which she'd so trustingly intertwined with mine. Something called my attention. Discreetly, carefully, I turned my hand so that I could see her thumb under mine. It was oddly thin and small, as if it belonged to a different, more childish hand, the hand of a little girl. I realised that she'd opened her eyes and was looking at me. She tried to remove her hand but I gripped it and stroked her thumb with my own.

'Now you know my most shameful secret,' she said. 'I still suck my thumb at night.'

Chapter 6

When I woke the following morning Beth was gone. A little taken aback, I stared at the gentle hollow in the bed left by her body. I felt for my watch: it was ten o'clock. I leapt up as I'd arranged to meet Emily Bronson at the Institute before lunch and I still hadn't finished reading through her papers. Feeling a little strange, I packed my racket and tennis clothes into a bag. It was Thursday and I was due to play as usual that afternoon. Before leaving I glanced once more, disappointed, at the desk and the bed. I would have liked to find a note from Beth, even if only a short one, a couple of lines, and I wondered whether her disappearing without leaving a message was the message.

It was a warm, quiet morning and the previous day seemed distant and vaguely unreal. But when I went out to the garden Mrs Eagleton wasn't there tidying the flowerbeds,

39

and yellow police tape still surrounded the porch. On my way to the Institute I stopped at a newsagent on Woodstock Road to buy a paper and a doughnut. In my office, I switched on the coffee machine and opened out the newspaper on my desk. The news of Mrs Eagleton's death was the lead story in the local news pages, with a banner headline reading 'Former War Heroine Found Murdered'. There was a photo of a young, unrecognisable Mrs Eagleton and another of the front of the house with a police barrier and cars outside. The article mentioned that the body had been found by a lodger, an Argentinian mathematics student, and that the last person to see the widow alive was her only granddaughter, Elizabeth.

There was nothing in the piece that I didn't already know; the post-mortem, late last night, apparently hadn't shown anything new. There were details of the police investigation in a separate box. It was anonymous but, beneath the seemingly impersonal style, I immediately recognised the insidious tone of the reporter who'd interviewed me. He stated that the police were ruling out an attack by an intruder, even though the front door hadn't been locked at the time. Nothing in the house had been touched or stolen. They did apparently have one lead, which Inspector Petersen didn't wish to reveal. The reporter was in a position to suggest that the lead might incriminate 'close members of Mrs Eagleton's family'. And he went straight on to say that Beth was the only immediate relative and would inherit 'a modest fortune'. In any case the article concluded, until there were any new developments, the *Oxford Times* echoed Inspector

Petersen's advice that householders should forget the good old days and keep their doors locked at all times.

I turned the pages, looking for the obituaries. There was a long list of names after Mrs Eagleton's obituary, including the British Scrabble Association and the Mathematical Institute, in which Emily Bronson and Seldom were both mentioned. I tore out the page and put it in a desk drawer. I poured another cup of coffee and immersed myself for a couple of hours in my Director of Studies' papers. At one o'clock I went downstairs to her office and found her eating a sandwich, with a paper napkin laid out over her books. She gave a little cry of delight when I opened the door, as if I had just returned safely from a dangerous expedition. We talked about the murder for a few minutes and I told her what I could, but didn't say anything about Seldom. She seemed dismayed and genuinely concerned about me. She hoped the police hadn't bothered me too much. They could be very unpleasant with foreigners, she said. She seemed to be on the verge of apologising for suggesting that I rent a room at Mrs Eagleton's. We talked for a little longer, while she finished her sandwich. She held it with both hands, pecking at it neatly like a little bird.

'I didn't realise Arthur Seldom was in Oxford,' I said at one point.

'I don't think he ever left!' said Emily with a smile. 'Like me, Arthur believes that if one waits long enough, all mathematicians end up making a pilgrimage to Oxford. He has a permanent position at Merton. But he doesn't show his face much. Where did you come across him?'

'I saw his name in the Institute's death notice,' I said cautiously.

41

'I could arrange for you to meet him, if you'd like. I think he speaks very good Spanish. His first wife was Argentinian,' she told me. 'She worked as a restorer at the Ashmolean, on the great Assyrian frieze.'

She broke off, as if she'd inadvertently been indiscreet.

'Did she . . . die?' I ventured.

'Yes,' said Emily. 'Years ago. She was killed in the same accident as Beth's parents. They were all four of them in the car. They were such close friends. They were on their way to Clovelly for the weekend. Arthur was the only one who survived.'

She folded the napkin and threw it into the wastepaper basket, taking care not to drop any crumbs. She took a sip from a little bottle of mineral water and adjusted her glasses on the bridge of her nose.

'Well now,' she said, peering at me with eyes that were a faded, almost whitish blue. 'Have you had time to read my papers?'

It was two o'clock by the time I left the Institute, carrying my tennis racket. It was the first truly hot day and the streets seemed to be asleep beneath the summer sun. A red double-decker Oxford Tour Guides bus turned the corner in front of me, as slowly and heavily as a slug. It was full of German tourists wearing sun visors and caps and pointing admiringly at the red building of Keble College. In the University Parks students were having picnics on the grass. I was overcome by a strong feeling of disbelief, as if Mrs Eagleton's death had already vanished. Imperceptible murders, Seldom had said. But really, any murder, any death barely ruffled the waters, quickly becoming imperceptible. Less than twenty-four hours had passed and it was as if nothing had been disturbed. Wasn't I myself now on my way to play tennis, as I did every Thursday? And yet, as I followed the curving path that led to the tennis club, I noticed an unusual stillness, as if small changes had secretly taken place after all. I could hear only the rhythmic striking of a solitary ball against a wall, with its magnified booming echo.

Neither John's nor Sammy's car was in the car park, but Lorna's red Volvo was parked on the grass beside the wire fence of one of the courts. I circled the changing room building and found her practising her backhand against the wall with intense concentration. Even from a distance I could appreciate the beautiful line of her firm, slim legs beneath the very short tennis skirt, and see her breasts tensing and protruding as she swung the racket for each shot. She stopped when she saw me and smiled, as if to herself.

'I thought you weren't coming,' she said. She wiped her forehead with the back of her hand and kissed me quickly on the cheek. She looked at me with an intrigued smile, as if she wanted to ask me something, or we were part of a conspiracy in which we were both on the same side but she didn't know her role.

'What happened to John and Sammy?' I asked.

'I don't know,' she said, innocently opening wide her big green eyes. 'Nobody called me. I was starting to think you'd all decided to abandon me.'

I went to the changing rooms and changed quickly, pleasantly surprised by this unexpected piece of luck. All the courts were empty. Lorna was waiting for me by the gate. I lifted the bolt and she went in ahead. In the short distance to the bench she turned to look at me again, hesitating. At last she said, as if she couldn't help herself:

'I read about the murder in the paper.' Her eyes shone almost with enthusiasm. 'My God, I knew her,' she said, as if she were still surprised, or as if it should have protected poor Mrs Eagleton. 'I saw her granddaughter in hospital a couple of times too. Is it true you found the body?'

I nodded as I took the cover off my racket.

'Promise you'll tell me all about it afterwards,' she said.

'I had to promise I wouldn't say anything,' I said.

'Really? That makes it even more interesting. I knew there was something else!' she exclaimed. 'It wasn't her – the granddaughter – was it? I'm warning you,' she said, pressing her finger into my chest, 'you're not allowed to keep anything secret from your favourite doubles partner. You'll have to tell me.'

I laughed, and handed her a ball over the net. In the silent, deserted club we started hitting shots from the back of the court. There's only one thing better in tennis than a hard-fought point, and that's the initial knock-up from the baseline where, conversely, you try to keep the ball in play as long as possible. Lorna was wonderfully confident on both forehand and backhand, and she held her own, staying near the lines until she found an opening for a drive, counter-attacking from the corner with an angled shot.

We played aiming the ball just within reach, increasing the pace with every shot. Lorna put up a brave defence, leaving long skid marks as she scrambled from one side of the court to the other, her efforts growing increasingly frantic. After each point she went back to the middle, breathing hard, flicking her ponytail behind her shoulder with a charming movement. She was facing the sun and her long, tanned legs gleamed beneath her skirt. We played in silence, concentrating, as if something more important were being settled on the court. During one of our longer points, she was running back to the centre of the court after hitting a sharply angled shot when she had to turn awkwardly to reach my return with her backhand. As she twisted, one of her legs gave way and she fell heavily sideways. She lay still, on her back, her racket some distance from her.

Worried, I ran to the net, but she wasn't hurt, just exhausted. She was out of breath, arms outstretched, as if she simply didn't have the strength to get up. I jumped over the net and crouched down beside her. She looked at me, her green eyes sparkling strangely in the sun, both mocking and expectant. I lifted her head and she raised herself up on one elbow, slipping her other arm around my neck. Her mouth was very close to mine and I felt her warm, still laboured breath. I kissed her and she fell back, taking me with her. We moved apart for a moment and looked at each other with the first deep, happy, slightly surprised look of lovers. I kissed her again and felt her breasts pressing against my chest. I slid my hand under her t-shirt and she let me stroke her nipple for a moment, but then she stopped me, alarmed, when I tried to slip my other hand under her skirt.

'Wait, wait,' she whispered, glancing around. 'Do you make love on tennis courts in your country?' She laced her fingers in mine to move my hand away gently and gave me another quick kiss. 'Let's go to my flat.' She stood up, rearranging her clothes and shaking the clay dust from her skirt. 'When you get your things, don't shower,' she whispered. 'I'll wait for you in the car.'

She drove in silence, smiling to herself and turning her head slightly to look at me from time to time. At a set of traffic lights, she stretched out her hand and stroked my face.

'So the matter of John and Sammy . . .' I said.

'I had nothing to do with it,' she said, laughing, but she sounded less convincing than earlier. 'Don't mathematicians believe in coincidences?'

We parked in a little sidestreet in Summertown and climbed the two floors up to Lorna's place, which was the attic flat of a large Victorian house. She opened the door and we started kissing again as soon as we were inside.

'I'm going to the bathroom for a minute, OK?' she said and headed along the corridor towards a door with a frosted-glass pane.

I waited in the small sitting room and looked around. It was charmingly untidy, full of a motley assortment of possessions – holiday snaps, soft toys, film posters and a large number of books crammed into a small bookcase. I leaned over to read some of the titles. They were all crime novels. I glanced in at the bedroom. The bed was neatly made, with a floor-length bedspread, and an open book lay face down on the bedside table. I went to take a look. I read the title and name above it, frozen with astonishment: it was Seldom's book on logical series, full of furious underlining and illegible notes in the margins. I heard the sound of the shower and, a little later, Lorna padding along the corridor in bare feet and her voice calling me. I put the book back as I found it and went to the sitting room.

'So,' she said from the door, showing me that she was already naked, 'still got your trousers on?'

Chapter 7

'There's a difference between the truth and the part of the truth that can be proved. In fact this is one of Tarski's corollaries to Gödel's theorem,' said Seldom. 'Of course, judges, pathologists, archaeologists all knew this long before mathematicians. Think of any crime with only two possible suspects. Both of the suspects know the part of the truth that matters, i.e. *it was me* or *it wasn't me*. But the law can't get to that truth directly; it has to follow a laborious, indirect route to gather evidence: interrogations, alibis, fingerprints and so on. All too often there isn't enough evidence to prove either one suspect's guilt or the other suspect's innocence. Basically, what Gödel showed in 1930 with his Incompleteness Theorem is that exactly the same occurs in mathematics. The mechanism for corroborating the truth that goes all the way back to Aristotle and Euclid, the proud machinery that starts from true statements, from irrefutable first principles, and advances in strictly logical steps towards a thesis – what we call the axiomatic method – is sometimes just as inadequate as the unreliable, approximative criteria applied by the law.'

Seldom paused for a moment and leaned over to the neighbouring table for a paper napkin. I thought he was going to write out a formula on it, but he simply wiped his mouth quickly and went on: 'Gödel showed that even at the most elementary levels of arithmetic there are propositions that can neither be proved nor refuted starting from axioms, that are beyond the reach of these formal mechanisms, and that defy any attempt to prove them; propositions which no judge would be able to declare true or false, guilty or innocent. I first studied the theorem as an undergraduate, with Eagleton as my tutor. What struck me most – once I had managed to understand and above all *accept* what the theorem was really saying – what I found so strange, was that mathematicians had got by perfectly well, without upsets, for so long, with such a drastically mistaken intuition. Indeed, at first, almost everyone thought that Gödel must have made a mistake and that someone would soon show that his proof was flawed. Zermelo abandoned his own work and spent two whole years trying to disprove Gödel's theorem. The first thing I asked myself was, why do mathematicians not encounter, and why over the centuries had they not encountered, any of these undecidable propositions? Why, even now after Gödel, can all the branches of mathematics still calmly follow their course?'

We were the last two people left at the long Fellows table at Merton. Facing us in an illustrious row hung portraits of distinguished former alumni of the college. The only name I recognised on the bronze plaques beneath the portraits was T.S. Eliot. Around us, waiters discreetly cleared away the plates of dons who had already gone back to their lectures. Seldom grabbed his glass of water before it was removed and had a long drink before continuing.

'In those days I was a fervent Communist and was very impressed by a sentence of Marx's, from *Contributions to the Critique of Political Economy*, I think, which said that historically humanity has only asked itself the questions it can answer. For a time I thought this might be the kernel of an explanation: that in practice mathematicians might only be asking the questions for which, in some partial way, they had proof. Not, of course, unconsciously to make things easier for themselves but because mathematical intuition – and this was my conjecture – was inextricably linked with the methods of proof, and directed in a Kantian way, shall we say, towards what can either be clearly proved or clearly refuted. That the knight's leap involved in the mental operations of intuition were not, as was often believed, sudden dramatic illuminations but modest, abbreviated versions of what could always be reached eventually with the slow, tortoise-like steps of a proof.

'I met Sarah, Beth's mother, at that time. She had just started studying physics and she was already engaged to Johnny, the Eagletons' only son. The three of us would go bowling or swimming together. Sarah told me about the uncertainty principle in quantum physics. You know what I'm referring to, of course: that the clear, tidy formulas governing physical phenomena on a large scale, such as the motion of celestial bodies, or the collision of skittles, are no longer valid in the subatomic world of the infinitesimal, where everything is far more complex and where, once again, logical paradoxes even arise. It made me change direction completely. The day she told me about the Heisenberg Principle was strange, in many ways. I think it's the only day of my life that I can recall hour by hour. As I listened, I had a sudden intuition, the knight's leap, so to speak,' he said, smiling, 'that exactly the same kind of phenomenon occurred in mathematics, and that everything was, basically, a question of scale. The undecidable propositions that Gödel had found must correspond to a subatomic world, of infinitesimal magnitudes, invisible to normal mathematics. The rest consisted in defining the right notion of scale. What I proved, basically, is that if a mathematical question can be formulated within the same "scale" as the axioms, it must belong to mathematicians' usual world and be possible to prove or refute. But if writing it out requires a different scale, then it risks belonging to the world – submerged, infinitesimal, but latent in everything – of what can neither be proved nor refuted. As you can imagine, the most difficult part of the work, and what has taken up thirty years of my life, has been showing that all the questions and conjectures that mathematicians from Euclid to the present day have formulated can be rewritten at scales of the same order as the systems of axioms being considered. What I proved definitively is that normal mathematics, the maths that our valiant colleagues do every day, belongs to the "visible" order of the macroscopic.'

'But that's no coincidence, I think,' I interrupted. I was

trying to link the results that I had presented at the seminar with what I was now hearing and find where they fitted in the large figure that Seldom was now drawing for me.

'No, of course not. My hypothesis is that it is profoundly linked to the aesthetic that has been promulgated down the ages and has been, essentially, unchanging. There is no Kantian forcing, but an aesthetic of simplicity and elegance which also guides the formulation of conjectures; mathematicians believe that the beauty of a theorem requires certain divine proportions between the simplicity of the axioms at the starting point, and the simplicity of the thesis at the point of arrival. The awkward, tricky part has always been the path between the two – the proof. And as long as that aesthetic is maintained there is no reason for undecidable propositions to appear "naturally".'

The waiter returned with a pot of coffee and filled our cups. Seldom remained silent for a time, as if he was unsure whether I'd followed what he was saying, or was perhaps a little embarrassed at having talked so much.

'What I was most struck by,' I said, 'the results that I presented in Buenos Aires, were in fact the corollaries that you published a little later on philosophical systems.'

'Actually, that was much easier,' said Seldom. 'It's the more or less obvious extension of Gödel's Incompleteness Theorem: any philosophical system which starts from first principles will necessarily have a limited scope. Believe me, it was much easier piercing through all the philosophical systems than through that single thought matrix to which mathematicians have always clung. Because all philosophical systems are simply too ambitious. Basically, it's all a question of balance: tell me how much you want to know and I'll tell you with how much certainty you'll be able to state it. But at the end, when I'd finished and I looked back after thirty years, it seemed that that first idea that Marx's sentence had suggested to me hadn't been so misguided after all. It had ended up, as the Germans would say, both eliminated from and included in the theorem. Indeed, a cat doesn't simply assess a mouse, it assesses it as a prospective meal. But the cat doesn't assess all animals as prospective meals, only mice. Similarly, historically, mathematical reasoning has been guided by a criterion, but that criterion is, deep down, an aesthetic. I found this to be an interesting and unexpected substitution with regard to necessity and a priori Kantians. A condition that is less rigid and possibly more elusive, but which also – as my theorem had shown – was substantial enough to be able, still, to say something and split waves. As you see,' he said, almost apologetically, 'it isn't easy to be free of such an aesthetic: we mathematicians always like to feel that we're saying something that is meaningful.

'However that may be, I have devoted myself ever since to studying what I privately call the aesthetic of reasoning in other spheres. I began, as always, with what seemed like the simplest model, or at least the closest: the logic of criminal investigations. I found the parallels with Gödel's theorem very striking. In every crime there is undoubtedly a notion of truth, a single true explanation among all the possible explanations. On the other hand, there are also material clues, facts that are incontrovertible or at least, as Descartes would say, beyond reasonable doubt: these would be the axioms. But then we're already in familiar territory. What is a criminal investigation if not our old game of thinking up conjectures, possible explanations that fit the facts, and attempting to prove them correct? I began systematically reading about real-life murders, I went through public prosecutors' reports for judges, I studied the method of assessing evidence and of structuring a sentence or an acquittal in a court of law. Just as when I was a teenager, I read hundreds and hundreds of crime novels. Gradually I began to find a multitude of interesting little differences, an aesthetic inherent in criminal investigations. And errors, too. I mean theoretical errors in criminology, which were potentially much more interesting.'

'What kind of errors?'

'The first, and most obvious, is attaching too much importance to physical evidence. Just think of what's happening now in this investigation. If you recall, Inspector Petersen sent one of his officers to retrieve the note I received. Here once again the same insurmountable gap opens up, between that which is true and that which is provable. I saw the note, and that's the part of the truth that the police can't get to. My statement isn't much use as far as police procedure goes; it doesn't carry the same weight as the little piece of paper itself. Now, the officer, Wilkie, completed his task as conscientiously as he could. He questioned Brent and got him to go over what he knew several times. Brent clearly remembered seeing a piece of paper folded in two at the bottom of my wastepaper basket, but it hadn't occurred to him to read it. Brent remembered too that I'd asked him if there was any way of retrieving the paper, and he told Wilkie what he told me: that he'd tipped the contents of the basket into an almost full refuse bag, which he'd put out soon after. By the time Wilkie arrived at Merton, the refuse lorry had been and gone almost half an hour earlier. When Petersen called me yesterday to ask me to describe the handwriting to their artist, I could tell that he was very disappointed at not finding the note. He's considered to be the best police inspector we've had in years. I've had a look at the complete notes to several of his cases. He's thorough, meticulous, implacable. But he's still an inspector. I mean, he was trained in accordance with police procedure: you can predict the way his mind is going to work. Unfortunately, people like him follow the principle of Ockham's Razor: as long as there's no physical evidence to the contrary they always prefer a simple hypothesis to a more complicated one. That's the second error. Not just because reality tends to be naturally complicated but mainly because, if the murderer really is intelligent and has prepared the crime carefully, he'll leave a simple explanation for all to see, a smokescreen, like a conjuror leaving the stage. But in the stingy logic of the economy of hypothesis a different reasoning prevails: why assume something strange and out of the ordinary, such as a murderer with intellectual pretensions, if they have more immediate explanations to hand? I could almost physically feel Petersen step back and re-examine his hypotheses. I think he would have started suspecting me, if he hadn't already checked that I was teaching between one and three that afternoon. I expect they checked out your statement too.'

'Yes. I was in the Bodleian Library when it happened. They went to enquire about me there yesterday. Luckily, the librarian remembered me because of my accent.'

'So you were consulting books at the time of the murder?' Seldom raised his eyebrows sardonically. 'For once, knowledge really is freedom.'

'Do you think Petersen will pounce on Beth now? She was terrified yesterday after they questioned her. She thinks the inspector is after her.'

Seldom thought for a moment.

'No, I think Petersen is cleverer than that. But consider the dangers of Ockham's Razor. Suppose for a moment that the murderer, wherever he is, decides that he doesn't have a taste for murder after all, or that the business with the blood and the police getting involved have ruined his fun; suppose that, for some reason, he decides to disappear from the scene. I think Petersen would then go after Beth. I know he questioned her again this morning, but this may simply have been a diversionary tactic, or a way of provoking the murderer, acting as if they don't know about him, as if this were an ordinary case, a murder in the family, as the newspaper suggested.'

'But you don't really think the murderer is going to quit the game, do you?' I asked.

Seldom pondered my question much more seriously than I'd expected.

'No, I don't,' he said at last. 'I just think he'll try to be more . . . imperceptible, as we said before. Are you free at all now?' he asked, glancing at the dining room clock. 'Visiting hours at the Radcliffe Hospital are about to start, and I'm heading there. If you'd like to come along, there's someone there I'd like you to meet.'

Chapter 8

We went out through the gallery of stone arches at the back of the college. Seldom showed me the sixteenth-century Royal Tennis Court on which Edward VII played, which reminded me of a *pelota* court. We crossed the road and turned down what looked like a cleft between two buildings, as if a sword had miraculously sliced through the stone from top to bottom with a single long blow.

'This is a short cut,' said Seldom.

He walked fast, slightly ahead of me because there wasn't room for both of us in the passageway. We emerged on to a path along the river.

'I hope you don't find hospitals too intimidating,' he said. 'The Radcliffe can be a little depressing. The building has seven floors. Perhaps you've heard of an Italian writer, Dino Buzzati? He wrote a story called exactly that, 'Seven Floors', based on something that happened to him when he was here in Oxford to give a lecture. He describes the experience in one of his travel diaries. It was a very hot day and, as he came out of the lecture hall, he fainted briefly. As a precaution, the organisers insisted he be checked out at the Radcliffe. He was taken up to the seventh floor, the floor reserved for minor cases and general check-ups. They examined him and carried out a few tests. They told him everything looked fine but they wanted to do some more specialised tests, just in case. For that, they had to take him down a floor; meanwhile, his hosts could wait for him upstairs. He was taken down in a wheelchair, which he found a little excessive, but he decided to put it down to British zeal. Along the corridors and in the waiting rooms on the sixth floor, he saw people with burnt faces, people wrapped in bandages, lying on trolleys, blind, mutilated. He himself was made to lie on a trolley while he was X-rayed. He was about to sit up when the radiologist said they'd detected a small anomaly – probably nothing serious, but he should remain lying down until they got the results of the other tests. He'd have to be kept under observation for a few more hours, so he'd be taken down to the fifth floor, where he could have a room to himself.

'On the fifth floor the corridors were empty but a few doors were ajar. Inside one of the rooms he glimpsed people lying in bed, arms connected to drips. He was left alone in a room, on a trolley, growing increasingly alarmed, for several hours. At last, a nurse came in, carrying a little tray containing a pair of scissors. She'd come to cut off some of the hair from the back of his head, on the instructions of a doctor on the fourth floor, Dr X, who would be carrying out the final examination. As his hair fell into the little tray, Buzzati asked if the doctor would be coming up to see him. The nurse smiled, as if only a foreigner could have thought such a thing, and said that the doctors preferred to remain on their own floors. But she would take him downstairs herself and leave him waiting beside a window. The building is U-shaped and, looking down from the window on the fourth floor, Buzzati could see the blinds at the first-floor windows which he describes in his short story. Some of the blinds were up, but most were pulled down. He asked the nurse who was on the first floor and she gave him the reply that he reproduces in the story: only the priest worked down on that floor. Buzzati writes that during the dreadful hour that he spent waiting for the doctor, he became obsessed with a mathematical idea. He realised that the fourth floor was exactly halfway in the countdown from 7 to 1 and, out of superstitious terror, he was convinced that if he went down one more floor, everything would be lost. Intermittently, from the floor below, he could hear what sounded like the desperate cries of someone delirious with pain and grief. It was as if the screams were creeping up the lift shaft. Buzzati decided to resist with all his might if they came up with any excuses for taking him down another floor.

'The doctor arrived at last. It wasn't Dr X but Dr Y, the consultant. He could speak a little Italian and he knew Buzzati's work. He took a quick look at the test results and the X-rays and expressed surprise that his young colleague, Dr X, should have given instructions to cut Buzzati's hair. Perhaps, said Dr Y, he was considering a preventive puncture. Anyway, it wouldn't be necessary. Everything was absolutely fine. The doctor apologised and said he hoped that Buzzati hadn't been too upset by the man screaming on the floor below. He was the only survivor of a car accident. The third floor could be very noisy, the doctor told him, a lot of the nurses down there used earplugs. But they would probably soon be taking the poor man down to the second floor and things would be quiet again.'

Seldom nodded towards the large, dark brick form that now rose before us. He went on, as if struggling to finish the story in the same calm, measured tone: 'The entry in Buzzati's diary is dated 27 June 1967, two days after the car crash in which I lost my wife, the crash in which John and Sarah died. The man in agony on the third floor was me.'

Chapter 9

We mounted the stone steps at the entrance in silence. Inside, we crossed a large hall. Seldom greeted almost all the doctors and nurses we passed in the corridors.

'I spent almost two years in here,' he said. 'And I had to come back every week for a whole year after that. Sometimes I still wake in the middle of the night thinking I'm back in one of the wards.' He indicated a bend in the corridor from which rose the worn steps of a spiral staircase. 'We're going to the second floor,' he said. 'It's quicker this way.'

On the second floor we walked down a long, bright corridor in which a deep, hushed silence reigned, as in a cathedral, and our steps echoed dismally. The floors looked as if they had just been polished, and shone as if few people ever walked across them.

'The nurses call this the Fish Tank, or the Vegetarian

Section,' said Seldom, pushing open the swing doors to one of the wards.

There were two rows of beds, with far too little space between them, as in a field hospital. In each bed there was a body of which you could see only the head, connected to an artificial respirator. The combined sound of the respirators was a deep, restful gurgling, which really did make you think of an underwater world. As we walked down the aisle between the rows of beds I noticed that a bag collecting faeces hung from the side of each body. Bodies, I reflected, reduced to nothing more than orifices. Seldom caught my expression.

'Once, I woke up in the night,' he whispered, 'and I heard two nurses, who'd been on duty in this ward, whispering about the "dirty ones" who filled their bags twice a day, so the nurses had the extra job of changing them again in the afternoon. Whatever their state, "dirty ones" don't last long on the ward. Their condition somehow always deteriorates slightly and they have to be transferred elsewhere. Welcome to the land of Florence Nightingale. The medical staff enjoy almost complete impunity because relatives rarely get this far – they visit once or twice in the beginning, then they disappear. It's like a warehouse. A lot of these patients have been on respirators for years. I try to get here every afternoon because, unfortunately, Frankie has recently become a "dirty one" and I wouldn't want anything strange to happen to him.'

We stopped by one of the beds. The man, or what remained of the man lying there, was a skull with a few grey hairs straggling over the ears and an impressively swollen vein at the temple. The body beneath the sheets had wasted away, making the bed seem far too big, and I suspected he might not have any legs. The thin white sheet hardly moved over his chest and, though the wings of his nose quivered, no breath misted the plastic mask over his face. One arm lay outside the sheet, connected by a copper fastening to what I thought at first must be a machine monitoring his pulse. In fact it was a device which held the arm in place over a notepad. A short pencil was attached rather ingeniously between the thumb and index fingers. But the hand, with very long nails, lay limp and lifeless on the sheet of white paper.

'Perhaps you've heard of him,' said Seldom. 'He's Frank Kalman. He extended Wittgenstein's work on rule-following and language games.'

I said politely that the name was familiar, though only very vaguely.

'Frank wasn't a professional logician,' said Seldom. 'In fact he was never the kind of mathematician who wrote papers or attended conferences. Soon after graduating he took a job in a large employment consultancy. His work involved preparing and assessing tests for applicants to various jobs. He was assigned to the department dealing with symbol manipulation and IQ tests. A few years later he was also appointed to set the first standardised tests in British secondary schools. He spent his whole life preparing logical series, of the most basic kind, like the one I showed you: given three symbols in sequence, please fill in the fourth symbol. Or series of numbers: given the numbers 2, 4, 8, please write the next number in the series. Frank was meticulous, obsessive. He used to check the mountains of tests one by one, and he started to notice something very odd. There were, of course, perfect exam scripts, about which you could say, as Frank wrote later with wonderful tact, that the candidate's answers exactly matched the examiner's expectations. There were also, and these were in the overwhelming majority, those Frank called the normal bell-curve – exam scripts with a few mistakes that belonged to the category of expected errors.

'But there was a third group, always the smallest, which drew Frank's attention. These were almost perfect exam scripts, in which all but one of the answers were the expected ones. But they differed from the usual cases in that the mistake in that single different answer seemed, at first glance, utterly absurd, a continuation picked almost blindly or at random, truly well outside the spectrum of usual mistakes. Out of curiosity, Frank thought of asking the candidates in that small group to justify their answers, and that was when he got his first surprise. The answers that he had considered incorrect were in fact another possible and perfectly valid way of continuing the series, only with a much more complicated justification. The strange thing is that these candidates hadn't seen Frank's elementary solution, and instead had jumped well beyond it, as if on a springboard. The springboard image is Frank's as well; he thought of the three symbols or numbers written on a paper as the diver's run along the diving board. Seen like that, the analogy seemed to provide him with an initial explanation: the farthest solution comes more naturally to a mind used to taking big leaps forward than the one that's right in front of it. But this, of course, challenged, at their very roots, the assumptions on which he'd based his life's work.

'Frank was suddenly disconcerted. The solutions to his series weren't in any way unique. Answers that he had so far considered wrong might be alternative and also, in some way, "natural" solutions. He couldn't even see a way of distinguishing between what might be a random answer and the continuation of a series which an exceptional, and too athletic, mind might choose. It was at this stage that he came to see me and I had to break the bad news to him.'

'Wittgenstein's finite rule paradox,' I said.

'Exactly. Frank had rediscovered in practice, in a real experiment, what Wittgenstein had already proved theoretically decades earlier: the impossibility of establishing an unambiguous rule. The series 2, 4, 8, can be continued with the number 16, but also with the number 10, or 2007. You can always find a justification, a rule, that lets you use any number as the fourth term in the series. *Any* number, *any* continuation. This is something Inspector Petersen wouldn't be too pleased to hear, and it almost drove Frank mad. He was over sixty by then, but he asked me for the references and he had the courage to enter, as if he were a student again, the abandoned cave that is Wittgenstein's work. And you know about Wittgenstein's descent into darkness. At one stage Frank felt as if he were on the edge of an abyss. He realised he couldn't even trust in the rule of multiplying by two. But he emerged with an idea, rather similar to my own. Frank clung with almost fanatical faith to the remains of the shipwreck: the statistics from his experiments. He believed that Wittgenstein's results were theoretical, from a Platonic world, but that real people thought in a different way. After all, only a tiny proportion came up with the atypical answers. So he conjectured that, though in principle all answers were equally probable, there might be something engraved on the human psyche, or in the approval-disapproval games during symbol learning, which guided most people to the same place, to the answer that seemed the simplest, clearest or most satisfying. He was definitely thinking, as I was, that some kind of aesthetic principle was operating a priori which only let through a few possible answers for the final choice. So he decided to provide an abstract definition of what he called normal reasoning.

'But he took a rather strange route. He started visiting psychiatric hospitals and trying out his tests on lobotomised patients. He collected examples of individual words and symbols written by people in their sleep. He took part in hypnosis sessions. But mainly he studied the types of symbols that brain-damaged patients in quasi-vegetative states used in attempts to communicate. Actually, he was trying to do something which by definition is almost impossible: to study what remains of reason when reason is no longer there watching over things. He thought he might be able to detect some kind of residual movement or stirring which corresponded to an organically imprinted track or routine pathway created by the learning process. I suppose he already had a morbid inclination which had something to do with what he was planning. He had just found out that he was suffering from a very aggressive form of cancer which first attacks the legs. All doctors can do is cut off limbs one after the other. I came to see him after the first amputation. He seemed to be in good spirits, considering the circumstances. He showed me a book his doctor had given him, containing photographs of skulls partially destroyed in accidents, suicide attempts, or smashed by bats. There was a comprehensive clinical account of the consequences and interconnections arising from brain injuries. Looking very mysterious, he pointed out a page which showed the left hemisphere of a brain with the parietal lobe partially destroyed by a bullet. He told me to read what it said below the photograph. The man, who had tried to commit suicide, had fallen into an almost complete coma, but for months his right hand had apparently kept drawing all kinds of strange symbols. Frank explained that, during his visits to hospitals, he had found a close connection between the type of symbols he was collecting and the occupation of the coma patient during their lifetime.

'Frankie was extremely shy, and this was the only time he confided anything of a personal nature: he told me he regretted never having married and, with a sad smile, he said he hadn't done much with his life, but he had drawn and manipulated logical symbols for forty years. He was sure he would never find a better subject than himself for his experiment. He was convinced that it would somehow be possible to read the coded residue or substratum that he'd been looking for in the symbols that he would draw. In any case he didn't intend to be around when they came for his other leg. But he had one last problem to solve, and that was how to ensure that the bullet didn't cause too much damage, that metal shards didn't reach the nerve circuits affecting motor function. I'd become fond of him over the years and I told him that I wasn't prepared to help him with his plan, so he asked if I'd be there to read the symbols, in the event that he succeeded.'

We both suddenly noticed the hand tense spasmodically, gripping the pencil, as if receiving electric shocks. Fascinated and horrified, I watched the pencil move slowly and clumsily across the page, but Seldom seemed not to pay much attention.

'He starts writing at this time of day,' he said, not bothering to lower his voice, 'and he continues almost all night. Anyway, Frankie was highly intelligent, he found the solution. An ordinary gun, even a small-calibre one, would leave too great a margin of error because of possible bullet fragments. He needed something that could penetrate the skull and reach the brain cleanly, like a small harpoon. This wing of the hospital was undergoing building work at the time and it seems he got the idea from a workman with whom he had a conversation about tools. In the end, he used a nail gun.'

I leaned forward to try to make out the confused marks appearing on the paper.

'Until recently his handwriting was perfectly legible, but it's becoming increasingly hard to read,' said Seldom. 'In fact he's only writing four letters, over and over again. The four letters of a name. All these years Frankie has never drawn a single logical symbol or number. The only thing he writes, endlessly, is a woman's name.'

Chapter 10

'Could we go out into the corridor for a moment? I need a cigarette,' said Seldom. He tore the page Frank had just written from the pad and, after glancing at it, threw it in a wastepaper bin. We left the ward quietly and walked down the empty corridor until we found an open window. We watched as a male nurse slowly wheeled a trolley towards us. As he passed, I saw a body shrouded in a sheet, with its face covered. Only an arm remained outside. There was a tag hanging from the wrist with a name on it and underneath I could just make out some numbers which may have been the time of death. The nurse skilfully manoeuvred the trolley, turning and sliding it through a narrow doorway with ease.

'Is that the morgue?' I asked.

'No,' said Seldom. 'There's a room like it on every floor. When a patient dies, the body is immediately moved out of the ward so as to free up the bed. The doctor in charge of the floor comes and confirms that the patient is dead and writes out a certificate. The patient is then transferred to the hospital morgue, which is in the basement.' Seldom nodded in the direction of Frank Kalman's ward. 'I'm going to stay and keep Frankie company a little longer. It's a good place to think. Well, as good as any. But I'm sure you'd like to visit the X-ray department,' he said with a smile. When he saw my surprise, his eyes twinkled and his smile grew even wider. 'Oxford's a small place, you know. Anyway, congratulations, Lorna's great. I met her some years ago, during one of my annual checkups. She lent me a good number of her crime novels. Have you seen her collection?' He raised his eyebrows in awe. 'I've never known anyone with such a fascination with crime. You have to go to the top floor,' he said. 'Take that lift there on the right.'

The lift went up with a heavy hydraulic moan. I walked through a maze of corridors, following the arrows to the X-ray department, until I came to a waiting room where a man with a faraway look was sitting, a book lying forgotten on his lap. Through a glass partition I caught sight of Lorna in her uniform, leaning over a bed. She seemed to be patiently explaining something to a child. I moved a little closer to the glass, but couldn't quite bring myself to interrupt her. She placed a teddy bear on the pillow. The child in the bed was a pale little girl of about seven, with frightened but alert eyes and long ringlets spread out over the pillow. Lorna spoke again and the child hugged the teddy bear tightly. I tapped gently on the partition. Lorna looked up, laughed with surprise and said something I couldn't hear through the glass. She indicated the door at the side and then, to the child, mimed, with an imaginary racket, that I was her tennis partner. She opened the door, gave me a quick kiss and asked me to wait for a moment.

I went back to the waiting room. The man was now reading his book. He had stubble on his chin and reddened eyes, as if he hadn't slept in a long time. With some surprise, I made out the title of his book: *From the Pythagoreans to Jesus*. The man suddenly lowered the book and met my eyes.

'I'm sorry,' I said, 'my attention was drawn by the title of your book. Are you a mathematician?'

'No,' he said, 'but since you're interested in the title I assume that you are.'

I smiled, nodding. The man stared at me with disconcerting intensity.

'I'm reading backwards,' he said. 'I want to know how things were in the beginning.' Again, he fixed me with his slightly fanatical gaze. 'I'm discovering surprising things. For instance, how many sects, or religious groups, would you say there were in Christ's time?'

I assumed it would be polite to venture a very small number but, before I'd had a chance to answer, the man went on:

'There were dozens and dozens,' he said. 'The Nazarenes, the Simonites, the Phibionites. Peter and the Apostles were only a tiny group. A tiny group among a hundred. Things could easily have been very different. They weren't the most numerous, or the most influential, or the most advanced. But they had a shrewd streak that made them stand out from the rest; a single idea, a touchstone that enabled them to pursue and eliminate all other groups

71

until they were the only ones left. While everybody spoke only of the resurrection of the soul, they promised the resurrection of the flesh as well. Coming back to life with one's own body. An idea which already sounded ridiculous and was already primitive in those days. Christ rose from the tomb on the third day and asked to be pinched and ate some grilled fish. Now, what happened to Christ during the forty days that he was back?'

His hoarse voice had the somewhat fierce vehemence of the autodidact or the recently converted. He was leaning towards me slightly and an acrid, penetrating smell of sweat wafted from his crumpled shirt. I moved back involuntarily, but it was difficult to escape his fixed stare. I shook my head in appropriate ignorance.

'Exactly,' he said. 'You don't know, I don't know, nobody knows. It's a mystery. All he seems to have done is be pinched and name Peter as his successor on earth. Rather convenient for Peter, don't you think? Did you know that until then corpses were simply wrapped in shrouds. There was no notion of preserving the body. It was, after all, what religion considered the weakest, most ephemeral part, the part vulnerable to sin. Well, nothing but a few wooden coffins separates us from those times. There's a whole world of coffins beneath this one. On the outskirts of every city there's another underground city of coffins, neatly lined up, lids affectingly closed. But we all know what happens inside. In the first twenty-four hours, after rigor mortis, the body starts to dry out. The blood stops transporting oxygen, the cornea turns cloudy, the iris and pupils become distorted, the skin shrivels. On the second day, the large intestine starts to putrefy, and the first green patches appear on the skin. The internal organs have shut down, tissues become soft. The third day, as decomposition progresses, gas bloats the abdomen and the limbs take on a green, marbled appearance. A compound of carbon and oxygen emanates from the body, the same penetrating smell you get from a steak left out of the fridge too long. Corpse fauna, including necrophagous insects, begins to feed on the body. Each of these processes, each exchange of energy, involves an irreversible loss; there is no way a vital function can be recovered. By the end of the third day, Christ would have been a monstrous piece of waste incapable of sitting up, foul-smelling and blind. That's the truth. But who's interested in the truth?

'You've just seen my daughter,' he said, and his voice was suddenly full of anguish and despair. 'She needs a lung transplant. We've been waiting for a donor for a year, she's on the emergency transplant list. She's got a month to live at most. Twice now we've had a possible donor. Twice I've pleaded and begged. But both times the families were Christian and they wanted to give their children a Christian burial.' He looked at me hopelessly. 'Do you know that under British law it's forbidden for the organs of parents who've committed suicide to be transplanted into their children? That's why,' he said, tapping the book cover, 'it's interesting sometimes to go back to the beginning of things. The ancients had other ideas on transplants. The Pythagoreans believed in the transmigration of souls . . .'

The man broke off and stood up. The door opened and Lorna came through pushing a bed. The little girl seemed to have fallen asleep. The man exchanged a few words with Lorna, then left, pushing the bed down the corridor. Lorna stood waiting for me to come to her, with an enigmatic smile and her hands in her pockets. Her apron, of a very fine fabric, was stretched pleasingly tight over her bust.

'What a lovely surprise,' she said.

'I wanted to see you in your nurse's uniform.'

She raised her arms seductively, as if she were going to turn and show off her uniform, but she only let me kiss her once.

'Any new developments?' she asked, wide-eyed with curiosity.

'No more murders,' I said. 'I've just been to the second floor. Seldom took me to Frank Kalman's ward.'

'I saw you being cornered by Caitlin's father,' she said. 'I hope he wasn't too depressing. I suppose he told you about the Spartans, and was scathing about Christians. He's a widower and Caitlin is his only child. He's managed to get leave from his job, and for the past three months he's been here almost all the time. He reads everything he can lay his hands on about transplants. I think by now he's gone a bit . . .' – she tapped her temple – 'cuckoo.'

'I was thinking of going to London for the weekend,' I said. 'Why don't you come with me?'

'I can't this weekend, I'm on duty both nights. But come on, let's go to the cafeteria, I can give you a list of bed-and-breakfasts and places to visit.'

'I didn't know Arthur Seldom had been to your house,' I said as we made our way to the lift.

I looked at her with a casual smile and, after a moment, she smiled back amused.

74

'He came to give me a copy of his book. I could give you another list, of all the men who've been to my flat, but it would be much longer.'

When I got back to my room at Cunliffe Close I found the envelope I'd prepared for Mrs Eagleton under a notebook and I realised that I'd never paid Beth the rent. I packed enough clothes for the weekend into a bag and went upstairs with the money. From behind the front door Beth told me to wait a moment. When she opened, she looked relaxed and calm, as if she'd just had a long bath. Her hair was wet, she was barefoot and she was wearing a long dressing gown, tightly wrapped around her. She invited me into the sitting room. I barely recognised it – she'd changed the furniture, the curtains, the rug. The room looked much more intimate and quiet, with a sophistication that seemed inspired by some home décor magazine. Though now completely different, it still looked pleasant and simple. Mainly, I reflected, if she had intended to make every last trace of Mrs Eagleton disappear, she had certainly succeeded.

I told her I was going to London for the weekend and she said that she too was going away the following day, after the funeral, on a short tour with the orchestra to Exeter and Bath. I suddenly heard the sound of splashing water from the bathroom, as if a rather large person were getting out of the bath. Beth looked very uncomfortable, as if I had caught her out. I assumed she was remembering, at the same time as I was, the contempt with which she had spoken of Michael only two days earlier.

I took the bus to London and spent two days wandering

around the city, in pleasantly warm sunshine, a tourist happily lost. On Saturday I bought *The Oxford Times* and found a short announcement about Mrs Eagleton's funeral, together with a brief summary of events which did not, however, provide any new information. In the Sunday papers there was no mention of the case. In Portobello Road, thinking of Lorna, I chose a rather dusty though well-preserved copy of the memoirs of Lucrezia Borgia, before catching the last train back to Oxford. On Monday morning, still half-asleep, I left for the Institute.

At the end of Cunliffe Close there was an animal lying in the road. It must have been run over during the night. I had to stop myself from retching as I passed it. I'd never seen such an animal before. It looked like a type of giant rat but with a short tail, around which lay a pool of blood. Its head had been totally crushed, but the black snout remained. Where its belly had once been, the unmistakable bulge of what must have been its offspring protruded as if from a torn sack. I quickened my pace involuntarily, trying to escape what I'd seen and the violent, almost inexplicable horror that it had evoked in me. The entire way to the Institute I struggled to rid myself of the image. I went up the steps of the building as if reaching a refuge. As I pushed the revolving door I saw a piece of paper stuck to the glass with Sellotape. The first thing that caught my eye was the diagram of a fish, placed vertically, drawn in black ink, that looked like two overlapping parentheses. Above it, in letters cut from a newspaper, it said: 'The second of the series. Radcliffe Hospital, 2.15 p.m.'

Chapter 11

In the secretary's office I found only Kim, the new assistant. I motioned urgently for her to remove her earphones and made her follow me to the entrance. She stared at me in surprise when I asked her about the piece of paper stuck to the door. Yes, she'd seen it when she arrived, but hadn't given it much thought. She'd supposed it referred to a charity event for the Radcliffe – a series of bridge matches, or a fishing competition. She'd been intending to tell the cleaning lady to move it to the notice board.

Kurt, the night watchman, emerged from his room under the stairs, ready to go home. He approached us, looking worried that there might be a problem. The paper had been there since the previous day, he'd seen it as he arrived. He hadn't removed it because he'd assumed somebody had authorised it before he came on duty. I said we ought to call the police and that someone should stay there to make sure nobody touched the glass panes of the revolving door or removed the paper as it might be linked to Mrs Eagleton's murder.

I ran upstairs to my office and phoned the police station, asking to be put through to Inspector Petersen or Detective Sergeant Sacks. I was asked my name and the number I was calling from and told to wait. After a couple of minutes Petersen came on the line. He let me speak without interrupting, at the end simply getting me to repeat what the night watchman had said. I realised that, like me, he thought another murder had already taken place. He said he'd send an officer and the fingerprints examiner to the Institute straight away. Meanwhile he'd go to the Radcliffe to check if anybody had died there yesterday. He'd want to talk to me again afterwards, and also, if possible, to Professor Seldom. He asked if we'd both be at the Institute. I said that, as far as I knew, Seldom should be about to arrive: there was a notice in the hall for a lecture at ten o'clock by one of his graduate students. It suddenly occurred to me that the piece of paper might have been stuck on the door for Seldom to see as he arrived. Perhaps, said Petersen, for him and another hundred mathematicians. He suddenly sounded uncomfortable. 'We can talk about it later,' he said, ending the call quickly.

When I went back down to the entrance hall, Seldom was standing by the revolving door. He was staring at the piece of paper with the little drawing of the fish as if he couldn't take his eyes off it.

'Are you thinking what I'm thinking?' he asked when he saw me. 'I'm afraid to ring the hospital and enquire about Frank. Although the time doesn't make sense,' he said, looking more hopeful. 'When I went to the hospital yesterday at four, Frank was alive.'

'We could call Lorna from my office,' I said. 'She's on duty till midday; she must still be there. She can easily find out.'

Seldom agreed and we went upstairs. I let him make the call. After being passed from department to department, he was eventually put through to Lorna. He asked her cautiously if she'd mind going down to the second floor and seeing if Frank Kalman was all right. I realised that Lorna was asking questions; I couldn't make out the words but I could hear her intrigued tone at the other end of the line. Seldom said only that a message had appeared at the Institute and that he was rather worried about it. And yes, it was likely that the message had something to do with Mrs Eagleton's murder. They talked for a little longer. Seldom told her that he was in my office and that she could call him there once she'd been down to check on Frank.

He hung up and we waited in silence. Seldom rolled a cigarette and stood at the window to smoke. At one point he turned round, went to the blackboard and, deep in thought, slowly drew the two symbols: first the circle, then the fish in two short curved strokes. He stood motionless, chalk in hand, head bowed, every so often making small futile marks at the edge of the board.

It was almost half an hour before the phone rang. Seldom listened to Lorna in silence, his face inscrutable, occasionally answering monosyllabically. 'Yes,' he said at last, 'that's exactly the time it says on the message.'

79

When he hung up and turned to me he looked relieved for a moment.

'It wasn't Frank,' he said, 'it was the patient in the next bed. Inspector Petersen has just been to the hospital morgue to check on the deaths that occurred on Sunday. The man who died was very elderly, over ninety. He was reported dead at two-fifteen yesterday, from natural causes. Apparently, neither the nurse nor the doctor in charge on that floor noticed a small dot on his arm, like the mark left by an injection. They're going to do a post-mortem on him now to find out what it is. But I think we were right. A murder that nobody considers a murder at first. A death that's believed to be from natural causes and a dot on an arm, that's all. An almost imperceptible dot. The murderer must have chosen a type of substance that doesn't leave any trace. I'm sure they won't find anything in the post-mortem. The dot is all that distinguishes this death from a death from natural causes. A dot,' repeated Seldom quietly, as if that were the starting point for a multitude of as yet invisible implications.

The phone rang again. It was Kim, from downstairs, telling me that a police inspector was on his way up to my office. I opened the door as Petersen's tall, thin frame appeared at the top of the stairs. He was alone and was visibly annoyed. He came into the office and, as he was greeting us, caught sight of the two symbols Seldom had drawn on the blackboard. He sat down abruptly.

'There's a crowd of mathematicians down there,' he said, almost accusingly, as if we were somehow to blame. 'The press will be here any minute. We'll have to tell them part of the story, but I'm going to ask them not to mention the first symbol of the series. Wherever possible we try to avoid publicising details of serial murders, particularly the recurring features. Anyway,' he said, shaking his head, 'I've been to the Radcliffe. This time it was a very elderly man called Ernest Clarck. He'd been in a coma, connected to a respirator, for years. He didn't have any family, apparently. The only link we can find so far with Mrs Eagleton is that Clarck, too, played a part in the war effort. But of course the same goes for any other man his age: that generation has the war years in common. The nurse found him dead during her rounds at two-fifteen and that was the hour she noted on his wristband, before moving him from the ward. Everything seemed perfectly normal – there were no signs of violence, nothing out of the ordinary. She took his pulse and wrote "death from natural causes", because she thought it a routine case. She said she couldn't understand how somebody could have got into the ward, because visiting hours were only just starting.

'The head doctor on the second floor admitted that he hadn't checked the body thoroughly. He'd arrived at the hospital late, it was a Sunday and he wanted to get home as quickly as possible. But above all, they'd been expecting Mr Clarck to die for months, in fact they were surprised that he was still alive. So he trusted the nurse's notes, copied the time and cause of death as they appeared on the label on to the death certificate and approved the transfer of the body to the morgue. I'm now awaiting the results of the post-mortem. I've just seen the note on the door downstairs. I suppose it was too much to expect that he'd use his own handwriting again, now that he knows we're after him. But it definitely makes things more difficult. Judging by the typeface I'd say he cut the letters from the *Oxford Times*, possibly even from articles about Mrs Eagleton. But the fish has been drawn by hand.' Petersen turned towards Seldom. 'What was your instinct when you saw the note? Do you think it's from the same person?'

'Difficult to say,' answered Seldom. 'It looks like the same type of paper, and the size of the symbol and its location on the page are similar. Black ink in both cases. Yes, in principle I'd say it was from the same person. I go to the Radcliffe almost every afternoon, to visit a patient on the second floor, Frank Kalman. Ernest Clarck was in the bed next to Frank's. Also, I don't come to the Institute that often but I did have to be here this morning. I think it's someone who's following my movements closely and knows quite a bit about me.'

'Actually,' said Petersen, taking out a small notebook, 'we're aware of your visits to the Radcliffe. You see,' he said apologetically, 'we had to make enquiries about you both. Now, let's see. You generally get to the Radcliffe around two in the afternoon, but this Sunday you got there after four. Why was that?'

'I was invited to lunch in Abingdon,' said Seldom. 'I missed the one-thirty bus back. There are only two buses on Sunday afternoons and I had to wait at the station until three.' Seldom searched one of his pockets and coldly held out a bus ticket to Petersen.

'Oh no, that's not necessary,' said the inspector, a little embarrassed. 'I was just wondering if . . .'

'Yes, I had the same thought,' said Seldom. 'I'm generally the first and only person to go into that ward during visiting hours. If I'd gone at my usual time, I'd have been sitting beside Mr Clarck's corpse the entire time. I assume that's what the murderer intended – that I'd be there when the nurse discovered that the man was dead during her round. But, again, things didn't turn out quite as he would have liked. In a way, he was too subtle: the nurse didn't see the needle mark on Clarck's arm, she thought he'd died of natural causes. And I arrived much later and didn't even notice that there was a different patient in the next-door bed. For me, it was an absolutely normal visit.'

'But perhaps he wanted the murder to be taken for a natural death at first,' I said. 'Maybe he prepared the scene so that the body would be removed before your eyes as if it were a routine death. In other words, that the murder should be imperceptible to you too. I think you should tell the inspector what you think,' I said to Seldom. 'What you told me earlier.'

'But we can't be sure yet,' said Seldom, his objection strictly intellectual. 'We can't make an induction with only two cases.'

'I'd like to hear your view anyway,' said Petersen.
Seldom still seemed unsure.

'In both cases,' he said at last, cautiously, anxious to keep to the facts, 'the murders were as slight as possible, if that's the right word. I don't think the deaths themselves are what really matters to him. The murders are almost symbolic. I don't believe that the killer is actually interested in killing, but in signalling something. Something that's undoubtedly linked with the series of figures he's drawn on the notes, beginning with a circle and a fish. The murders are simply a way of drawing attention to the series and he's choosing victims close enough to me so that I'll get involved. I think in fact that it's a purely intellectual problem, and that he'll only stop if we somehow manage to prove to him that we've determined the meaning of the series; in other words, that we can predict which symbol, or murder, comes next.'

'I'm going to get a psychological profile drawn up this afternoon, though I don't think we've got much to go on yet. But perhaps you can now answer the question I asked you before: do you think it's a mathematician?'

'I'm inclined to say no,' answered Seldom slowly. 'At least, not a professional mathematician. I think he's someone who imagines that mathematicians are paragons of intelligence and that's why he wants to challenge them directly. He's a sort of intellectual megalomaniac. I don't think it's a coincidence that he chose to place his second message on the Institute door. I assume there's a second hidden message to me in it: if I don't take up the challenge, another mathematician will. And if we're making conjectures, I'd say that it's someone who was once unjustly failed in a maths exam, or who missed an important opportunity in life because of an IQ test of the kind Frank Kalman devised. Someone who was excluded from what he considers the realm of intelligence, someone who both admires and hates mathematicians. Possibly he conceived the series as revenge against his examiners. In a way, he's the examiner now.'

'Could it be a student whom you failed?' asked Petersen.

Seldom smiled.

'I haven't failed anyone in a long time,' he said. 'I only

have graduate students now, and they're all excellent. I'm inclined to believe that it's someone who hasn't studied maths formally but who's read the chapter on serial murders in my book and, unfortunately, thinks that I'm the person he has to challenge.'

'Right,' said Petersen, 'as a first step, I can get a list of all the credit-card purchases of your book at the bookshops in town.'

'I don't think it'll be much help,' said Seldom. 'When the book first came out, my publishers managed to get the chapter on serial murders published in the *Oxford Times*. A lot of people thought it was a new kind of crime novel. That's why the first edition of the book sold out so fast.'

Petersen stood up, looking a little discouraged, and examined the two figures on the blackboard for a moment.

'Can you tell me anything more about this now?'

'The second symbol of a series generally provides a clue as to how the rest of the series should be read: whether as a representation of objects or facts from a possible real world – in other words, as symbols in the most usual sense – or, without any connotation of meaning, on a strictly syntactical level, as geometric figures. The choice of the second figure is, again, very clever because the fish is drawn in such a simplified style that it can be read both ways. The vertical position is interesting. It might be a series of figures symmetrical to the vertical axis. If we really are to interpret it as a fish, there are, of course, many other possibilities.'

'The fish tank,' I said, and Petersen turned to me, a little surprised. Seldom nodded.

'Yes, that's what I thought at first. That's what they call the floor Ernest Clarck was on at the Radcliffe,' he said. 'But that would point directly to someone inside the hospital, and I don't think he'd choose a symbol that would incriminate him so obviously. And anyway, if that's the case, what does the circle have to do with Mrs Eagleton?' Seldom paced up and down for a while, head bowed. 'Something else that's interesting,' he said, 'and which is implicit in a way in the notes, is that he assumes that mathematicians will be able to find the solution. In other words, there must be something in the symbols that matches the type of problems, or intuitions, related to a mathematician's way of thinking.'

'Would you like to venture what the third symbol might be?' asked Petersen.

'I have an initial idea,' said Seldom. 'But I can see several other ways the series might continue that are, shall we say, reasonable. That's why in tests you're given at least three symbols before you're asked what the next one is. Two symbols still allow too many ambiguities. I'd like to have more time to think about it. I wouldn't want to get it wrong. He's the examiner now and another murder would be his way of giving us another bad mark.'

'Do you really believe he'll stop if we find the solution?' asked Petersen doubtfully.

But there was no such thing as *the* solution, I thought. That was the most exasperating thing. I suddenly understood why Seldom had wanted to introduce me to Frank Kalman and the second dimension to the problem that was preoccupying him. I wondered how he'd explain minds that took big leaps, Wittgenstein, rule-following paradoxes and the movements of normal bell-curves to Petersen. But Seldom needed only one sentence:

'He'll stop,' he said slowly, 'if it's the solution that *he* has in mind.'

Chapter 12

Petersen stood up and paced about the room, his hands behind his back. He picked up his jacket – which earlier he'd laid on the edge of the desk – turned for a moment to stare at the blackboard, and wiped off the circle with his hand.

'Remember, as far as possible, we're going to keep the first symbol to ourselves. I don't want to tempt a copycat killer. Do you think any of the mathematicians downstairs might be able to guess the next symbol, now that they know the second?'

'No, I don't think so,' said Seldom. 'And I'm not sure they'd be interested enough to try. To a mathematician, the only problem that matters tends to be the one he's working on at the time. It may take more than a couple of murders to tear them away from what they're doing.'

'Does the same go for you?' Petersen was now staring

hard at Seldom; there was cold reproach in his voice. 'To be honest, I'm a little . . . disappointed,' he said, choosing his words carefully. 'I wasn't expecting you to give me a definitive answer today, of course, but I had hoped for four or five possible alternatives, conjectures that we could work on or eliminate. Isn't that how mathematicians work? But perhaps a couple of murders don't interest you enough either.'

'I have an initial idea, as I said,' said Seldom, his small pale eyes meeting the inspector's. 'I promise I'll give the matter my full attention. I just want to be sure that I'm not mistaken.'

'I wouldn't want you to wait until the next murder to find out if you were right,' said Petersen. Then, as if reluctantly trying to make up for his earlier sharpness, he went on: 'But if you really do want to help, please come to my office tomorrow, after six. We'll have the psychological profile by then. I'd like you to read it: it may bring someone to mind. You're welcome to come too,' he said to me, and quickly shook hands with both of us.

After Petersen had left there was a long silence. Seldom went to the window and started rolling a cigarette.

'Can I ask you a question?' I said at last cautiously. I was aware that he might not want to tell me anything either, but I decided it was worth a try. 'Your idea, your conjecture, is it about the next symbol, or the next murder?'

'I think I've got an idea about how the series continues – about the next symbol in the series,' said Seldom slowly. 'But it doesn't enable me to infer anything about the next murder.'

89

'All the same, wouldn't even that – the symbol – be a great help to Inspector Petersen? Is there any other reason why you don't want to tell him?'

'Come on, let's go for a walk in the park,' he said. 'I've got a few minutes before my student's lecture and I need a cigarette.'

There were policemen still at the entrance dealing with the fingerprints on the glass, so we left by one of the back doors. En route we passed Podorov. He greeted me half-heartedly and stared fixedly at Seldom, as if hoping Seldom would recognise him. We walked around the Physics Laboratory and took one of the gravel paths leading into the University Parks. Seldom smoked in silence, and I thought for a moment that he wasn't going to say anything more.

'Why did you become a mathematician?' he asked suddenly.

'I don't know,' I said. 'Perhaps it was a mistake. I always thought I'd do a humanities degree. I suppose what attracted me was the kind of truth that theorems contain: timeless, immortal, self-contained, and yet absolutely democratic. Why did you choose mathematics?'

'Because it harms no one,' said Seldom. 'Because it's a world that has nothing to do with reality. You know, terrifying things happened to me when I was very young, and have happened throughout my life, as if they were signs. They've been intermittent, but still too frequent and too terrible for me to ignore.'

'What type of signs?'

'Let's say . . . I noticed the chain of events provoked by any small action on my part in the real world. They were

90

probably coincidences – just unfortunate coincidences – but they were so devastating that they almost brought me to a complete standstill. The last of these signs was the accident in which my wife and two closest friends died. I don't know how to say this without sounding ridiculous but, from very early on, I noticed that the conjectures I made about the real world always came true, but by strange paths and in the most horrible ways, as if I were being warned that I should keep away from the world of people. I was utterly terrified during my adolescence. It was then that I discovered mathematics. For the first time in my life I felt I was on safe ground. For the first time I could follow a conjecture, as determinedly as I liked, and when I wiped the blackboard clean, or crossed out a page where I'd made mistakes, I could start again entirely from scratch, without unexpected consequences. There is a theoretical parallel between mathematics and criminology; as Inspector Petersen said, we both make conjectures. But when you set out a hypothesis about the real world, you inevitably introduce an irreversible element of action, which always has consequences. When you look in one direction, you stop looking in all the others. When you follow a possible path, you follow it in real time and it may then be too late to try a different one. What I most fear is not, as I told Petersen, getting it wrong. What I most fear is what has happened throughout my life: that what I'm thinking will come true in the most horrific way.'

'But saying nothing, refusing to reveal the symbol, is that not in itself, by omission, a form of action which might also have incalculable consequences?'

'Perhaps, but for now I'd rather take that risk. I'm not

as keen as you to play the detective. And if maths is demo-cratic, the next symbol in the series will be obvious to all. You, Petersen himself, you all have the necessary elements to find it.'

'No, no,' I objected, 'what I meant was that in maths there's a democratic moment, when the proof is set out line by line. Anyone can follow the path once it's been marked out. But there is of course an earlier moment of illumina-tion, what you called the knight's leap. Only a few people, sometimes only one person in many centuries, manage to see the correct first step in the darkness.'

'A good try,' said Seldom. '"One person in centuries" sounds very dramatic. Anyway, the next symbol I have in mind is very simple. It doesn't really require mathematical knowledge. But establishing the relationship between the symbols and the murders is more difficult. It may not be such a bad idea to have a psychological profile. Well,' he said, glancing at his watch, 'I should head back to the Institute.'

I said I wanted to walk on a bit further and he handed me the card that Petersen had given him.

'Here's the address of the police station. It's opposite a shop called Alice in Wonderland. We could meet there at six, if that suits you.'

I continued along the path and stopped in the shade of some trees to watch the unfathomable mystery of a game of cricket. For several minutes I thought I was witnessing the preparatory stages before the game, or else a series of failed attempts to start. But then I heard enthusiastic applause from some women in large hats sitting drinking punch at one end of the field. I'd obviously missed a wonderful piece of play. Perhaps the game had reached a decisive moment just then, before my very eyes, but all I could see was an exasperating lack of action.

I crossed a small bridge – on the other side, the park lost some of its neatness – and walked along the river through yellowing pastureland. Every so often I saw couples in punts on the river. There was an idea somewhere there, close by, like the buzzing of an insect that you can't see, an intuition about to be clarified, and for a moment I felt that if I were in the right place perhaps I'd be able to glimpse an edge and grab hold of it. As in maths, I wasn't sure whether to persist and try to conjure it up, or forget about it, deliberately turn away and wait for it to appear of its own accord. Something in the tranquillity of the landscape, the gentle splashing of oars hitting water, the polite smiles of the students in the passing boats, seemed to dilute the tension. In any case it wasn't here, I realised, that the key to deaths and murders would be revealed to me.

I took a short cut through the trees back to my office. My Russian colleague had gone to lunch, so I decided to ring Lorna. She sounded cheerful and excited. Yes, she had *news*, but first she wanted to hear mine. No, Seldom had told her only that a strange message had appeared stuck to a window. I told her how I had found the note, described the symbol and then repeated as much as I could remember of the conversation with Inspector Petersen. Lorna asked a few more questions before telling me what she knew: Ernest Clarck's body hadn't been transferred to the police morgue; instead, the police pathologist had carried out the post-mortem at the hospital, with one of the doctors there. She'd managed to get the doctor to tell her about it over lunch. 'Was that difficult?' I asked with a pang of jealousy. Lorna laughed. Well, he'd invited her to sit at his table several times before, and this time she'd accepted.

'Both he and the pathologist were nonplussed,' said Lorna. 'Whatever Mr Clarck was injected with, it left no trace – they found absolutely nothing. The doctor said he too would have signed a certificate stating it was a death from natural causes. Now, there could be an explanation: there's a fairly new drug, extracted from the mushroom *Amanita muscaria*, and no reagent to detect it has yet been found. It was presented last year at a closed medical conference in Boston. The strange thing – the most interesting thing – is that forensic pathologists have never publicised the existence of the drug. Apparently, they all swore never even to reveal its name. Wouldn't that indicate that the police should look for the murderer among forensic pathologists?'

'Or among the nurses who have lunch with them,' I said. 'As well as the secretaries who took the minutes at the conference, the chemists and biologists who identified the chemical and maybe the police too. They must have been informed of the drug's existence.'

'Well, anyway,' said Lorna, offended, 'it narrows down the search: it's not something you find in any bathroom cabinet.'

'That's very true,' I said, trying to sound placatory. 'Shall we have dinner together this evening?'

'I can't, I'm working late, but how about tomorrow? Six-thirty at the Eagle and Child?'

I remembered my appointment with Inspector Petersen.

'Could we make it eight? I'm still not used to having supper so early.'

Lorna laughed.

'OK, we can keep your *gaucho* hours for once.'

Chapter 13

A policewoman so gaunt that she almost disappeared inside her uniform led us upstairs to Inspector Petersen's office. We entered a large room, with walls a strong salmon-pink, which retained a proud British post-war austerity, quite devoid of luxury. There were several tall metal filing cabinets and a surprisingly modest wooden desk. From the window you could see a bend of the river and, in the protracted summer light, students lying on the bank catching the last of the sun. The still, golden water made me think of the paintings by Roderic O'Conor that I'd seen in London, at the Barbican Gallery.

Here in his office, leaning back in his chair, Petersen looked more relaxed, less watchful. Or perhaps he simply no longer considered us suspects and wanted to show us that he could, if he chose, exchange his policeman's mask for the usual British mask of politeness. He got up and brought us a couple of severe high-backed chairs, upholstered in a fabric that was shiny with wear and coming unstitched at the corners. As he sat down again, I noticed a silver frame on a corner of the desk: it contained a photograph of a young Petersen helping a little girl on to a horse. From what Seldom had told me about him, I had expected to see piles of documents, newspaper cuttings, maybe some photos on the walls of cases he had solved. But, in that perfectly anonymous office, it was impossible to tell if Petersen was an exemplar of modesty, or simply the kind of person who prefers not to give away too much about himself so that he can find out everything about others. He opened a desk drawer and took out a pair of glasses, which he slowly wiped with a cloth. He glanced at some pages on his desk.

'Right,' he said, 'I'll read you the main points of the report. Our psychologist seems to think the murderer is a man, of around thirty-five. In the report she refers to him as Mr M, presumably for "murderer". M, she tells us, is probably from a lower-middle-class family, from a village or the suburbs of a town. He may have been an only child, but at any rate he was a child who excelled early in an intellectual pursuit, such as chess, or maths, or reading, which was something unusual in his family. His parents mistook his precociousness for genius, and it meant that he didn't participate in the games and rituals of other children his age. He may have been a target for their teasing and things may have been made worse by some sign of physical weakness, such as a girlish voice, or glasses, or being overweight. The teasing made him even more withdrawn and caused him to entertain his first fantasies of revenge.

In these fantasies, typically, M imagines that he triumphs over his enemies with his talent and success, crushing those who've humiliated him.

'At last, the day of the test arrives, the moment he's been waiting for for so many years – a particularly important contest of some kind or exam in the area he has excelled in. It's his big opportunity, his chance to escape his background and start the other life he's been preparing for, silently, obsessively, his entire adolescence. But something goes terribly wrong, the examiners are unfair in some way and M returns, defeated. This causes the first crack. It's called the Ambère Syndrome, after the writer in whom this type of obsession was first observed.'

Petersen opened a drawer and brought out a thick volume on psychology. A little strip of paper marked a place a few pages in. 'I thought it might be interesting to go over this first case. Let's see: Jules Ambère was a penniless, obscure French writer. In 1927, he sent the manuscript of his first novel to the publisher G . . ., then the leading publisher in France. He'd worked on the novel for years, rewriting it obsessively. Six months went by before he received an unquestionably polite letter from one of the editors, a letter he kept until the very end. In the letter, the editor expressed her admiration for his novel and suggested that he come to Paris to discuss the terms of a contract. Ambère pawned his few possessions of value to pay for the journey, but at the meeting something went wrong. They took him to lunch at a smart restaurant, where his clothes looked out of place, he had poor table manners, he choked on a fish bone. Nothing too serious, but the contract didn't get signed and Ambère returned to his village humiliated. He started carrying the letter around in his pocket and, for months, repeated the story endlessly to his friends. The second recurring feature of the syndrome is this period of incubation and fixation, which can last several years. Some psychologists call it the "missed opportunity" syndrome, to emphasise this feature: the injustice occurs at a decisive moment, a turning point which could have drastically altered the person's life. During the incubation period the person returns obsessively to that one moment, unable to resume his previous life, or else he readjusts, but only outwardly, and he begins to have homicidal fantasies.

'The incubation period ends when what is referred to in psychological literature as the "second opportunity" arises, a conjunction which partially recreates that first event, or seems sufficiently similar. Many psychologists here draw a parallel with the tale of the genie in the bottle in *The Thousand and One Nights*. In Ambère's case the second opportunity was particularly clear-cut, but the pattern is often more vague. Thirteen years after his rejection, a reader who had only just joined the publisher G . . . came across the manuscript by chance as they were moving offices, and the author was summoned to Paris for a second time. This time Ambère was impeccably turned out, watched his manners throughout the meal, made sure his conversation was casual and cosmopolitan and, once the pudding was served, strangled the woman at the table before the waiters had a chance to stop him.'

Petersen raised an eyebrow and closed the book. He glanced at the next page of the psychologist's report in silence before putting it aside, and quickly scanned the first few paragraphs of the third page.

'The report continues here with what interests us. The psychologist maintains that we're not dealing with a psychopath. A psychopath typically exhibits a lack of remorse and a gradual increase in cruelty, combined with nostalgia – he's searching for something that will move him. But so far in this case, on the contrary, he's shown delicacy, a concern to do as little harm as possible. The doctor, like you,' he said, turning towards Seldom for a moment, 'seems to find this particularly fascinating. In her opinion, it was the chapter of your book on serial murders that provided M with the "second opportunity". Our man felt revived. He's seeking both admiration and revenge: admiration from the group to which he's always wanted to belong and from which he's been unjustly excluded. And here at least the psychologist does offer a possible interpretation of the symbols. In his fits of megalomania, M feels like a creator, he wants to name things again. He endlessly perfects his creation: as in Ecclesiastes, the symbols testify to the stages in his development. The next symbol, she suggests, could be a bird.'

Petersen gathered together the pages and looked at Seldom.

'Does any of this chime with your thoughts on the matter?'

'Not with regard to the symbol. I still believe that if the notes are addressed to mathematicians, the key must also in some way be mathematical. Is there any explanation in the report for the "slight" nature of the murders?'

'Yes,' said Petersen, leafing back through the pages. 'I'm

afraid the psychologist believes that the murders are a way of paying court to you. In M, a general desire for revenge is combined with a much more intense desire to belong to the world that you represent, to have the admiration – even horrified admiration – of those who have rejected him. That's why for now he's chosen a way of murdering which he thinks a mathematician would approve of – with a minimum of components, aseptic, without cruelty, almost abstract. As in the early stages of infatuation, M is trying to please you; the murders are offerings. The psychologist thinks that M may be a repressed homosexual who lives alone, but she doesn't discount the possibility that he's married and, even now, has a conventional family life masking his secret activities. She adds that if he gets no sign of a response, this initial seduction stage may be followed by a second, furious stage, in which the murders are more vicious, or target people much closer to you.'

'Well, this psychologist seems almost to know him personally. All that's missing is for her to tell us that he's got a mole on his left arm!' exclaimed Seldom. I wasn't sure if there was only sarcasm in his voice, or a hint of contained irritation as well. I wondered if he'd been shocked by the reference to homosexuality. 'I'm afraid that we mathematicians make much more modest conjectures. I have, however, given more thought to what you said and decided that I should maybe tell you my idea.' He took a small notebook from his pocket and, using a fountain pen from Petersen's desk, quickly drew a few strokes which I couldn't see. He tore out the page, folded it in two and handed it to Petersen. 'Here you have two possible continuations of the series.'

There had been something secretive in the way Seldom folded the paper that Petersen seemed to have caught. He looked at the paper in silence for a moment before folding it again and placing it in a desk drawer. He didn't ask Seldom any questions. Perhaps in the small duel the two men had engaged in, Petersen was satisfied for now – he had got Seldom to reveal the symbol and didn't want to bother him with more questions. Or perhaps he simply wanted to discuss it later with him in private. It occurred to me that maybe I ought to get up and leave, but it was Petersen who stood and saw us out with an unexpectedly friendly smile.

'Have you had the results of the second post-mortem?' asked Seldom as we headed towards the door.

'That's another interesting little mystery,' said Petersen. 'At first, the forensic pathologists were puzzled: they found no trace of any known poison in the body. They thought they might even be dealing with a very new drug that leaves no trace, of which I'd never heard. But I think I've solved this at least,' he said, and for the first time I saw something like pride in his eyes. 'The murderer may think he's very clever, but we policemen do a bit of thinking from time to time as well.'

Chapter 14

We left the police station in silence and walked back along St Aldates without a word until we reached Carfax Tower.

'I need to buy tobacco,' said Seldom. 'Would you like to come with me to the Covered Market?'

I nodded and we turned down the High. I hadn't said a word since we left the police station. Seldom smiled to himself.

'You're offended because I didn't tell you what the symbol was. But believe me, I have a very good reason.'

'A different reason from the one you gave me in the park yesterday? Now that you've shown it to Petersen, I can't see why there should be any adverse consequences of me knowing it.'

'There could be . . . other consequences,' said Seldom. 'But that's not exactly why I haven't told you. I don't want my conjectures to influence yours. It's what I do with my

103

graduate students: I try not to get ahead of them with my own reasoning. The most valuable time in a mathematician's thinking process is the moment when he has his first solitary intuition about a problem. Though you may not believe it, I have more faith in you than in myself to find the correct answer. You were there at the beginning, and the beginning, as Aristotle would say, is half of everything. I'm sure you noticed something, though you may not yet know what. And above all, you're not English. The first crime was the matrix. The circle is like the zero in natural numbers, a symbol of maximum uncertainty but which also determines everything.'

We entered the market and Seldom took his time choosing a tobacco mix at a tobacconist's run by a woman of Indian appearance. The woman, who got up from her stool to serve him, was wearing a saffron-coloured robe and an earring like a silver coil hung from her left ear. On closer inspection, I saw that it was in fact a snake. I suddenly remembered what Seldom had said about the ouroboros of the Gnostics and couldn't help asking the woman about the symbol.

Tapping the serpent's head, she said:

'Nothing and everything. The emptiness of every separate thing, and the totality that embraces them all. Difficult, difficult to understand. Absolute reality, beyond negation. Eternity, that which has no beginning and no end. Reincarnation.'

She carefully weighed out the tobacco and exchanged a few words with Seldom as she handed him his change. We made our way out through the maze of stalls. In the arcade, we saw Beth standing by a little table, handing out leaflets for the Sheldonian Orchestra. They were holding a charity concert and the members of the orchestra, she told us, took turns selling tickets. Seldom picked up one of the programmes.

'It's an orchestral concert at Blenheim Palace, with fireworks during one of the pieces,' he said. 'I'm afraid you can't leave Oxford without going, at least once, to a concert with fireworks. Allow me to buy you a ticket.' And he took the money for two tickets from his pocket.

I hadn't spoken to Beth since my trip to London. As she tore out the tickets and wrote the seat numbers, I had the feeling that she was avoiding my gaze. The meeting seemed to embarrass her.

'Will I get to hear you play at last?' I asked.

'It'll probably be my last concert,' she said, her eyes meeting Seldom's for a moment. She went on, as if this were something she hadn't told anyone yet and she wasn't sure he would approve: 'I'm getting married at the end of the month and I'm going to take some time off. I don't think I'll carry on playing afterwards.'

'That's a pity,' said Seldom.

'That I'm stopping playing or that I'm getting married?' asked Beth, and she smiled joylessly at her own joke.

'Both!' I said. They laughed openly, as if my answer had provided unexpected relief. As I watched them laughing, I remembered what Seldom had said about me not being English. There was something restrained even in this spontaneous laughter, as if it were an unaccustomed liberty and they shouldn't take it too far. Seldom could have objected that he was Scottish, of course, but even so, in their gestures, or rather in their careful economy of gestures, they had an undeniable air in common.

We emerged on to Cornmarket Street and I pointed out to Seldom a notice that I had seen earlier on one of the boards at the entrance to the Bodleian Library. It was for a round-table discussion in which Inspector Petersen and a local crime writer would be taking part: 'Is there such a thing as the perfect crime?' The title made Seldom stop for a moment.

'Do you think this is some kind of bait Petersen is putting out?' he asked. The thought hadn't occurred to me.

'No, the poster's been up for nearly a month. And I assume that if they were laying a trap for the murderer they would have invited you too.'

'*Perfect Crimes* . . . I consulted a book with that same title when I was trying to establish the parallels between logic and criminal investigations. The book cited dozens of cases that have never been solved. The most interesting, for my purposes, was the case of a doctor, Howard Green, who formulated the problem most precisely. He wanted to kill his wife and wrote a diary setting out, in a truly scientific, detailed manner, all the possible adverse ramifications. It would be easy, he concluded, to kill her in such a way that the police couldn't pin the blame on anyone with certainty. He proposed fourteen different methods, some highly ingenious. It would be much more difficult to ensure that he himself remained above suspicion forever.

'The real danger for a criminal, Green claimed, was not the investigation of events backwards in time – that was no problem as long as the murder was planned carefully enough, making sure all trails were blurred or erased –

but the traps that might be laid for him *going forwards in time*. The truth, he wrote in almost mathematical terms, is strictly unique; any deviation from the truth can always be refuted. At every interrogation, he would know what he had done, and in every alibi he devised there would inevitably be something false which, with sufficient patience, could always be exposed. He wasn't satisfied with any of the options he analysed – getting someone else to kill her, pretending it was suicide or an accident, and so on. He concluded that he would have to provide the police with another suspect, one who was obvious and immediate and who meant the case was closed. The perfect crime, he wrote, wasn't one that remained unsolved, but one where the wrong person was blamed.'

'Did he kill her in the end?'

'Oh no, *she killed him*. She found the diary one night and they had a terrible fight. She defended herself with a kitchen knife, stabbing and mortally wounding him. At least, that's what she told the court. The jury, horrified by the contents of the diary and photographs of the bruises on her face, decided that she acted in self-defence and found her innocent. It's because of her in fact that the murder is included in the book: many years after her death some students of graphology proved that the handwriting in the diary, while an almost perfect imitation, was not in fact Dr Green's handwriting. And they discovered another fascinating fact: the man she married discreetly shortly afterwards was a copyist of illustrations and ancient works of art. I'd like to know which of them penned the diary: it's a masterly imitation of the scientific style. They were incredibly daring, because the diary, which was read out during the trial, recounted and revealed line by line what they had done. Lying with the truth, with all one's cards on the table, like a conjuring trick performed with bare hands. By the way, have you heard of an Argentinian magician called René Lavand? If you see his act you never forget it.'

I shook my head – the name wasn't even vaguely familiar.

'No?' said Seldom, surprised. 'You must see his show. I know he's coming to Oxford soon, we could go together. Do you remember our conversation at Merton, about the aesthetics of reasoning in different disciplines? As I told you, the logic of criminal investigations was my first model. The second was magic. I'm glad you don't know him,' he said, with childlike enthusiasm. 'It'll give me an excuse to see his show again.'

When we arrived at the Eagle and Child I could see Lorna inside. She was sitting with her back to us, her red hair loose and flowing. She was absent-mindedly turning over a beer mat. Seldom, who had automatically brought out his packet of tobacco, followed my gaze.

'Go on in,' he said. 'Lorna doesn't like to be kept waiting.'

Chapter 15

Almost two weeks passed without my hearing anything more about the case. I also lost contact with Seldom, though I found out from a casual remark of Emily's that he was in Cambridge, helping to organise a seminar on Number Theory. 'Andrew Wiles thinks he can prove Fermat's last conjecture,' Emily said, amused, as if talking about an incorrigible child, 'and Arthur is one of the few people who's taking it seriously.' This was the first time I'd heard Wiles's name. I didn't think any professional mathematicians were still working on Fermat's last theorem. After three hundred years of struggle and especially since Kummer, the theorem was considered the paradigm of mathematical difficulty. At any rate, it was beyond all known mathematical tools, and so difficult it would consume the life and career of anyone who took up the challenge. When I said some of this to Emily, she agreed, as if she too found it mystifying. 'And yet,' she said, 'Andrew was my student, and if there's anyone in the world who can solve it, I'd put my money on him.'

During those weeks I accepted an invitation to a conference on Model Theory in Leeds but, instead of paying attention to the lectures, I found myself, during sessions, drawing circle and fish symbols in the margins of my notebook, like an invocation to the void. I'd tried to read between the lines of the newspaper articles that appeared in the days following Ernest Clarck's death but, perhaps because Inspector Petersen had intervened, a possible link between the two murders was only mentioned in passing. The fish symbol was described but the newspapers seemed unaware of its significance and inclined to believe it was a kind of signature. I'd asked Lorna to write in great detail if there were any new developments but, instead of a report, I received the kind of letter I thought people no longer wrote, and which I certainly never would have expected from Lorna. Long and tender, it was a love letter.

At the seminar someone was discussing the Chinese Room Experiment. I reread Lorna's words, which she seemed to have written in an unchecked fit of passion, reflecting that the burning question in translation was knowing – really knowing – what the other person meant when they slipped a page containing the terrible word under your door. In my reply I copied Qais ben-al-Mulawah's plea in one of his poems to Layla:

> Oh God, make the love between us equal
> that neither should go beyond the other

110

Make our loves identical
like two sides of an equation.

I returned to Oxford on the day of the concert. Seldom had left a note in my pigeonhole at the Institute containing a little map with directions, the different ways of getting to Blenheim Palace, and a time for us to meet. In the afternoon, as I was changing, there was a knock at my door. It was Beth. For a moment I couldn't say anything – all I could do was stare. She was wearing a low-cut black dress and matching long gloves. Her hair was tied back, showing off her elegant jawline, long, slender neck and bare shoulders. It was the first time I'd ever seen her wearing make-up and the transformation was spectacular. She smiled nervously as I stared at her.

'Michael and I wondered if you'd like us to give you a lift, if you don't mind arriving a little early. We're about to leave.'

I grabbed my thin cotton sweater and followed her out through the garden. I'd seen Michael only once before, from a distance, from my window. He was loading Beth's cello on to the back seat. When he looked up and said hello, I saw a cheerful, ingenuous face with ruddy cheeks that made him look like a countryman or happy beer drinker. He was tall and heavily built, but there was something soft about his features that reminded me of Beth's disparaging remark about him. His tailcoat was slightly crumpled and he couldn't quite button it across his middle. Lank blond hair flopped over his forehead, and I noticed that he flicked it back constantly. I reflected maliciously that he would probably soon be bald.

He started up the engine and manoeuvred the car slowly out of the close. As we came to the crossroads with the main road the headlamps lit up the crushed animal which was still lying in the road. Michael swerved to avoid it and lowered his window to look at the bloody remains. It was completely flattened but still, disturbingly, preserved its shape in two dimensions.

'It's a badger,' he said to Beth. 'It must have strayed out of the woods.'

'It's been there for days,' I said. 'I passed it when it had just been run over. I think it was carrying young. I'd never seen one before.'

Beth leaned over to Michael's side and glanced quickly out the window, without much interest.

'Isn't anybody going to clear away the remains?' I asked.

'No. The refuse collectors are superstitious. Nobody dares touch a badger, they think they bring bad luck. It'll gradually get worn away by the cars.'

Michael speeded up to get through the lights and, as we joined the flow of traffic, he starting asking me the usual polite questions. I recalled the words of an English writer – Virginia Woolf, I think – who had once excused the formality of her compatriots by explaining that the initial, apparently trivial, conversation about the weather served to establish common ground and a comfortable atmosphere before moving on to more important subjects. But I was starting to wonder if that second stage really existed, and if I'd ever get to hear about those more important subjects. At one point I asked them how they had met. Beth said that they sat next to each other in the orchestra, as if that explained everything, and in fact the more I watched them, that did indeed seem like the only explanation. Proximity, routine, repetition – a most effective combination. He hadn't even been, as some women say, 'the first to come by'; it was something more immediate: 'the one sitting nearest'. But what did I know? I didn't, of course, but I suspected that Michael's main attraction was that another woman had chosen him first.

We joined the ring road and, for a few minutes, as Michael accelerated on the dual carriageway and advertising hoardings flashed past, I felt I was back in the modern world. We turned off towards Woodstock down a narrow tree-lined road. The branches intertwined overhead, forming a long tunnel in which you could only see to the next bend in the road. We went through the small village, drove about two hundred metres down a side road and, passing under a stone arch, we saw, in the late-afternoon sun, the huge gardens, the lake and the majestic outline of the palace, with its gold spheres on the roof and marble figures peering down from the balustrades like lookouts. We parked near the entrance. Beth and Michael walked across the gardens carrying their instruments to the stage, where chairs and music stands were set out for the orchestra. The seats for the audience, as yet unoccupied, had been painstakingly arranged in perfect concentric semicircles. I wondered how long this small miracle of geometry would last once people started arriving and if anybody else would get to admire the effort. I decided to go for a walk through the woods and around the lake in the half-hour before the performance.

The light was fading. An elderly man in a grey uniform was rounding up the peacocks for the night. Through the trees, I glimpsed horses loose in a field. I passed a guard with two dogs and he tipped his cap in greeting. By the time I reached the lake it was dark. When I looked back towards the palace it was as if a giant switch had been flicked: the entire façade was lit up, brilliant and serene as an ancient jewel. Touched by the reflection, the lake stretched much further than I had thought, so I gave up on the idea of getting all the way round and doubled back.

A great many seats were now occupied and I was surprised by the number of people still arriving in groups, trailing perfume and long dresses. Seldom was waving his programme at me from a row near the front. He too looked unusually elegant, in a dinner jacket and black bow tie. We chatted for a while about the seminar he was organising in Cambridge, the secrecy surrounding Wiles's presentation and, very briefly, my trip to Leeds. I looked round and saw two ushers hurriedly unfolding chairs and setting out an extra row.

'I didn't expect so many people,' I said.

'Yes,' said Seldom, 'almost all of Oxford's here: look over there.' And he indicated with his eyes a place a few rows back to the right.

I turned as discreetly as I could and saw Inspector Petersen with a young woman, probably the fair-haired little girl from the photograph twenty years on. The inspector nodded to us.

'And there's someone else I now find everywhere I go,' said Seldom. 'Two rows back, the man in the grey suit pretending to read the programme. Do you recognise him out of uniform? It's Detective Sergeant Sacks. Petersen seems to think our man may try to strike closer to me next time.'

'So you've spoken to Inspector Petersen again?' I asked.

'Only on the phone. He asked me to write, as simply as possible, a justification for the third symbol, the law of formation of the series, as I see it. I sent him my explanation from Cambridge. It was barely half a page long, unlike that very . . . er . . . imaginative report he read us. I think he has a plan, but he probably still has some doubts. It's interesting how seductive a psychologist's conjectures can be. Even if they're incorrect or ridiculous, they're always more attractive than purely logical reasoning. People have a natural resistance to, and instinctive mistrust of logical thought. And even if it is completely mistaken, that resistance – as one sees if one studies the historical development of logic in the human mind – may have some foundation.'

Seldom had lowered his voice slightly. The murmur of conversation around us ceased and the lights dimmed. A powerful beam of white light dramatically illuminated the orchestra. The conductor tapped briefly on the music stand, pointed his baton at the lead violin and the solitary first line of the piece that opened the programme made its way tentatively in the silence, like a curl of smoke rising.

Gently, as if gathering delicate threads in the air, the conductor brought in Beth and Michael, the wind section, the piano and, lastly, the percussionist. I stared at Beth, although in fact I'd been watching her all along, even while listening to Seldom. I wondered if it was on stage that she felt her true connection with Michael. They both looked fully absorbed and focused, following the score, turning the pages briskly. Every so often a sudden strike of the drum would make me look up at the percussionist. Very tall, hunched with age, with a white moustache, slightly yellowed at the tips, that must once have been his pride and joy, he was by far the oldest member of the orchestra. When he wasn't playing he looked shaky and unsteady, in contrast to the spasmodic vigour with which he struck the drum, almost as if he were trying to hide the early stages of Parkinson's. I noticed that he put his hands behind his back after striking the drum and that the conductor was trying, rather comically, to get him to moderate his efforts. The music rose to a majestic climax and the conductor signalled the end of the piece with an energetic wave of his baton, before turning, with bowed head, to receive the first applause.

I asked Seldom for the programme. The next piece was Aaron Copland's *Cheyenne Spring*, the third of the series of seasons, for triangle and orchestra. I handed the programme back to Seldom and he glanced at it quickly.

'Perhaps we'll get the fireworks now,' he whispered.

I followed his gaze up to the palace roofs. Among the statues, you could make out the moving shadows of the men preparing the fireworks. Everything became quiet, the lights over the orchestra went out and a single spotlight focused on an elderly, ghostly figure holding up a triangle. We heard a distant, hieratic tinkling, like the dripping of thawing ice. The orchestra reappeared, bathed in a light tinged with orange, possibly intended to represent the dawn. The triangle sounded in counterpoint to the flutes, gradually fading from the central motif. In turn, other instruments joined in, putting one in mind of flowers slowly opening out. The conductor's baton suddenly set a frenzied rhythm for the brass, which sounded like wild horses galloping across the plains. Gradually all the sections of the orchestra submitted to the insane pace, until the conductor waved his baton in the percussionist's direction. The spotlight again focused on him, as if a crescendo was to come from there. But, in the harsh white beam, we could see that something was terribly wrong.

Still holding the triangle, the old man seemed to be gasping for air. He dropped the instrument, which struck a jarring note as it hit the ground, and staggered down from his platform. The spotlight followed him, as if the lighting technician couldn't take his eyes off the horrifying scene. The percussionist held out his arm towards the conductor in a mute plea for help, then raised both hands to his throat, as if defending himself from an invisible attacker who was trying to strangle him. He fell to his knees and there was a chorus of muffled screams, most of the people in the front row rising from their seats. Members of the orchestra surrounded the percussionist and called desperately for a doctor. A man made his way along our row and on to the stage. I stood to let him pass and couldn't help following him.

Inspector Petersen was already with the musicians and I saw that Detective Sergeant Sacks too had jumped up on to the stage, gun in hand. The percussionist lay face down in a grotesque pose, his hand still gripping his throat, his face a bruised blue, like a marine animal that had stopped breathing. The man who had pushed past me was a doctor.

117

He turned the body over, pressed two fingers to the neck to check the pulse and closed the eyes. Crouching beside him, Petersen discreetly showed him his ID card and spoke to him for a moment. He then made his way through the orchestra to the percussionist's platform and began searching the floor. The triangle was lying by the steps and he picked it up with his handkerchief. I turned and saw Seldom in the crowd behind me.

Petersen was motioning for Seldom to join him in one of the empty rows of seats. I pushed through the throng until I reached Seldom and followed him, but he seemed not to notice me. He said nothing and his expression was impossible to read. We made our way slowly back to our seats. Petersen had climbed down from the stage and was now approaching us from the opposite end of the row. Seldom stopped suddenly, frozen at the sight of something on his seat. Someone had torn a couple of phrases from the programme and formed a short message. I managed to read them before the inspector moved me aside. The first said: 'The third of the series.' The second was the word 'triangle'.

Chapter 16

Inspector Petersen motioned peremptorily to Sacks. The detective inspector, who had been standing guard over the body, made his way towards us through the crowd, showing his police badge.

'Don't let anyone leave,' ordered Petersen. 'I want the names of all the people here.' He took out his mobile phone and handed it to Sacks, together with a small notebook. 'Contact the car park attendant and make sure he doesn't let any cars out. And get a dozen officers here to take statements, another officer to watch the lake, and two more to intercept anyone who gets on to the road via the woods. I want you to do a head count of the audience and compare it with the number of tickets sold and seats occupied. Talk to the ushers and find out how many extra seats they set out. And I want another list that includes the palace staff, members of the orchestra and people organising the fireworks. One more thing,' he said as Sacks was about to leave. 'What were your orders this evening, Detective Sergeant?'

Petersen was staring at him severely and Sacks turned pale, like a student faced with a difficult question.

'To watch anyone who came near Professor Seldom,' he answered.

'In that case perhaps you can tell us who left this message on his seat.'

Sacks looked at the two little pieces of paper and his face fell. He shook his head despondently.

'I really thought someone was strangling that man, sir,' he said. 'That's what it looked like from where I was sitting: as if someone was trying to throttle him. I saw you take out your gun and I ran on to the stage to help him.'

'But he didn't die of strangulation, did he?' asked Seldom quietly.

Petersen seemed to hesitate a moment before answering.

'Apparently, it was spontaneous respiratory arrest. Dr Sanders, the doctor who went up on the stage, operated on him two years ago for pulmonary emphysema and gave him five or six months to live. It was a miracle he was still standing, his respiratory capacity was so reduced. The doctor's initial diagnosis is that the man died of natural causes.'

'Yes,' murmured Seldom, 'natural causes. It's remarkable how skilled he's becoming, isn't it? A natural death, of course, the logical extreme, the most perfect example of an imperceptible murder.'

Petersen took out his glasses and again leaned over the pieces of paper.

'You were right about the next symbol,' he said, looking up at Seldom. He still didn't seem sure whether the professor was an ally or adversary. I could understand why: there was something in Seldom's way of reasoning that was inaccessible to the inspector, and Petersen wasn't used to having someone one step ahead of him in an investigation.

'Yes, but as you can see, knowing it was no help.'

'There are a few strange differences from the other messages: this one doesn't have a time. And the strips of paper have ragged edges, as if they were torn out carelessly, and in a hurry, from the programme.'

'Perhaps,' said Seldom, 'that's exactly what he wants us to think. Wasn't the entire scene, with the spotlight and the climactic moment in the music, like a consummate magic act? In fact the death of the percussionist wasn't the important thing; the real trick was leaving these two bits of paper under our very noses.'

'But the man up there on the stage is dead. That's not a trick,' said Petersen coldly.

'Yes,' said Seldom, 'that's what's so extraordinary: the reversal of the routine, the major effect at the service of the minor effect. We still don't know what the figure is. We can draw it now, we can follow the outline, but we can't *see* it, at least, not yet as he does.'

'But if what you thought was right, showing him that we know the continuation of the series might be enough to stop him. Anyway, I think we've got to try – to send him a message right now.'

'But we don't know who he is,' said Seldom. 'How can you get a message to him?'

121

'I've been wondering about it since I received the little note with your explanation. I think I've got an idea. I'm hoping to ask the psychologist about it this evening and call you afterwards. If we want to get ahead of him and prevent the next murder, we've got no time to lose.'

We heard an ambulance siren and saw that an *Oxford Times* van had also drawn up. The passenger door opened and a photographer appeared, followed by the gangling reporter who had interviewed me at Cunliffe Close. Inspector Petersen carefully picked up the two little strips of paper by their edges and put them in his pocket.

'For the time being this is a natural death,' he said. 'I don't want that reporter to see me talking to you.' Petersen turned towards the crowd gathered round the stage. 'Right,' he said with a sigh, 'I've got to count all these people.'

'Do you really think he might still be here?' asked Seldom.

'I think whether the head count is complete or some-body's missing, we'll know something more about him.'

Petersen moved away a few steps and stopped to talk to the young woman who had been sitting beside him during the performance. The inspector motioned in our direction and the girl nodded. A moment later she headed resolutely towards us, with a friendly smile.

'My father said they won't be allowing any taxis or cars out for some time. But I'm heading back to Oxford now. I could drop you off somewhere.'

We followed her to the car park and got into a car with a discreet police identity badge on the windscreen. As we left the parking area we saw the two officers Petersen had requested.

'It's the first time I've managed to get my father to a concert,' said the woman. 'I thought it would take his mind off his work. Oh well, I suppose he won't be coming to dinner now. My God, that man holding his throat . . . I still can't believe it. Daddy thought someone was trying to choke him. He was about to fire at the stage but because the spotlight was on the man's face he couldn't see anything behind him. *He* asked *me* if he should fire.'

'What did you see from where you were sitting?' I asked.

'Nothing! It all happened so fast. And anyway, I was distracted, looking up at the palace. I knew the fireworks would be going off at the end of the movement so I was watching out for that. They always get me to organise the fireworks at these events. I suppose they think I know all about gunpowder because I'm a policeman's daughter.'

'How many people were up on the roof dealing with the fireworks?' asked Seldom.

'Two. That's all you need. There might have been one more person up there, at most – one of the palace security guards.'

'From what I could see,' said Seldom, 'the percussionist was slightly apart from the rest of the orchestra. He was the last person right at the back of the stage, up on a platform. He was the only member of the orchestra who could be attacked from behind without the others noticing. Someone from the audience or from the palace could have gone round to the back of the stage when the lights went down.'

'But my father said the cause of death was respiratory arrest. Could something like that be induced externally?'

123

'I don't know, I don't know,' said Seldom, and then added very quietly: 'I hope so.'

What did he mean? I was about to ask him, but the inspector's daughter had already drawn him into a conversation about horses, which then switched irretrievably and rather unexpectedly to a search for common Scottish ancestors. I turned his intriguing words over in my mind for a while, wondering if I'd missed a possible nuance in English of the expression 'I hope so'. I assumed that this had simply been his way of saying that the hypothesis about an attack was the only reasonable one, and that for the sake of general good sense it was better to assume that this was what had happened. That if the man's death had not been caused in some way, that if he really had died of natural causes, one could only think of something inconceivable: invisible men, Zen archers, supernatural influences. Strange how the mind automatically makes little alterations, adjustments: I convinced myself that that was what Seldom had meant and never asked him about it, either when we got out of the car or during any of our subsequent conversations. And yet I now realise that those quietly uttered words would have been the key, the short cut, into his deepest thoughts.

All I can say in my defence is that I was intent on something else: I didn't want to let Seldom escape that evening without him revealing the law of formation of the series. To my shame, even knowing the triangle symbol, I was as much in the dark as I had been at the start. Half-listening to the conversation in the front, I tried vainly to give some sense to the circle–fish–triangle sequence and imagine what the fourth symbol might be. I was determined to extract the answer from Seldom as soon as we got out of the car and was watching Petersen's daughter's smiles a little anxiously. Although the meaning of certain colloquial expressions escaped me, I realised that the conversation had become more personal and at one point she said again, in a forlorn tone intended to be alluring, that she would be having dinner alone that night. We took the Banbury Road into Oxford and the inspector's daughter stopped the car at the start of Cunliffe Close.

'This is all right here, isn't it?' she asked, with a charming but firm smile.

I got out of the car but before she drove off, on a sudden impulse I tapped at Seldom's window.

'You have to tell me,' I said in Spanish, quietly but urgently, 'even if it's only a clue, tell me something more about the solution to the series.'

Seldom looked at me in surprise, but my plea had worked and he seemed to take pity on me.

'What are we, you and I, what are we mathematicians?' he said, and smiled with strange melancholy, as if recovering a memory that he had thought lost. 'We are, as a poet from your country said, "the arduous disciples of Pythagoras".'

Chapter 17

I stood on the pavement watching the car disappear into the darkness. In my pocket, together with my room key, I had a key to the side door of the Institute and the swipe card for getting into the library out of hours. I decided that it was too early to go to bed, so I walked to the Institute in the yellowish glow of the street lights. The streets were empty; the only signs of movement I saw were in Observatory Street, through the window of a tandoori restaurant: two waiters were placing chairs on tables and a woman in a sari was closing the curtains. St Giles too was deserted, but there were lights in a few windows at the Institute and a couple of cars in the car park. Some mathematicians worked only at night, and others had to come back to check on the running of a long program.

I went upstairs to the library. The lights were on and, as I entered, I heard footsteps – someone was walking quietly among the bookshelves. I went to the History of Mathematics Section, and ran a finger along the titles. One book was jutting out, as if someone had looked at it recently and placed it back carelessly. The books were packed in tightly, so I had to pull it out with both hands. The illustration on the cover showed a pyramid consisting of ten points surrounded by fire. The title – *The Pythagorean Brotherhood* – was only just out of reach of the flames. From close up, the points were actually small shaven heads, as if they were monks seen from above. So perhaps, rather than being vaguely symbolic of the inflamed passions that geometry could arouse, the flames alluded specifically to the horrific fire which destroyed the sect.

I carried the book to one of the tables and opened it under the lamp. I didn't have to turn more than a couple of pages. There it was. It had been there all along, in all its overwhelming simplicity. The most ancient and elementary mathematical concepts, not yet quite divested of mysticism. The representation of numbers in the Pythagorean doctrine as the archetypal principles of divine powers. The circle was One, unity in all its perfection, the monad, the beginning of everything, enclosed and complete within its own line. Two was the symbol of multiplicity, of all opposition and duality, of bringing into being. It was formed by intersecting two circles, and the oval – like an almond – enclosed at its centre, was called *Vesica Piscis*, the belly of the fish. Three, the triad, was the union of two extremes, the possibility of bringing order and harmony to differences. It was the spirit that embraced the mortal and immortal within a single whole.

But also, One was the point, Two was the straight line joining two points, Three was the triangle and, at the same time, the plane. One, two, three: that was all, the series was simply the sequence of natural numbers. I turned the page to examine the symbol for Four. It was the *tetraktys*, the pyramid of ten points that was on the book's cover, the emblem and sacred figure of the sect. The ten points were the sum of one, plus two, plus three, plus four. It represented matter and the four elements. The Pythagoreans believed that all of mathematics was encoded in the symbol. It was both three-dimensional space and the music of the celestial spheres, and it contained in rudimentary form the combinatorial numbers of chance and the numbers of the multiplication of life that Fibonacci rediscovered centuries later.

I heard footsteps again, much closer. I looked up and to my surprise saw Podorov, my Russian room-mate, emerge from among the shelves. On seeing me at the table, he approached with an intrigued smile. It was strange how different he looked there, quite at home. I imagined he liked having the library to himself at night. He was holding a cigarette and he tapped it gently on the glass table top before lighting it.

'Yes,' he said, 'I come here at night so that I can smoke in peace.'

He gave me a wry but friendly smile and flipped over the book's cover to see the title. He was unshaven and his eyes were hard and shining.

'Ah, *The Pythagorean Brotherhood* . . . This has something to do with the symbols you drew on the board in our office, doesn't it? The circle, the fish . . . If I remember rightly, they're the sect's first symbolic numbers, aren't they?' He thought for a moment and recited, as if showing off his memory: 'The third one is the triangle, the fourth is the *tetraktys*.'

I looked at the man, amazed. I realised that Podorov, who'd seen me studying the two symbols on the blackboard, hadn't even considered that it might be anything other than a strange mathematical problem. Podorov, who obviously knew nothing about the murders, could, all along, have simply got up from his desk and drawn the continuation of the series on the board for me.

'Is it a problem that Arthur Seldom has set you?' he asked. 'It was from him that I first heard about these symbols, in a lecture he gave at a conference on Fermat's last theorem. You know, of course, that Fermat's theorem is simply an extension of the problem of the Pythagorean triples, the sect's best-kept secret.'

'When was that?' I asked. 'Not recently, surely.'

'No, no, it was years ago,' he said. 'So long ago that, as far as I can tell, Seldom doesn't remember me. Of course, he was already the great Seldom then, while I was just an obscure graduate student from the small Russian town in which the conference was held. I showed him my work on Fermat's theorem – it was all I thought about at the time – and I asked him to pass it on to the Number Theory group in Cambridge, but they were apparently too busy to read it. Well, not all of them,' he said. 'One of Seldom's students read my work, corrected my faulty English and published it under his own name. He was awarded the Fields Medal for the most important contribution of the decade to solving the problem. Now Wiles is about to take the final step thanks to those theorems. When I wrote to Seldom, he answered that there was an error in my work and that his student had corrected it.' Podorov laughed drily and exhaled a puff of smoke forcefully upwards. 'My only mistake,' he said, 'was that I wasn't English.'

I wished I had the power to make him stop talking. I felt again, as I had during my walk in the University Parks, that I was on the point of *seeing* something and that perhaps, if I were alone, the piece of the puzzle that had eluded me once would fall into place. I got up, murmuring a vague excuse, and quickly filled out a card so that I could borrow the book. I wanted to be outside, far away, in the night, away from everything. I rushed downstairs and, as I was heading out the door, I almost collided with a black-clad figure entering from the car park. It was Seldom, now wearing a raincoat over his dinner jacket. I suddenly realised it was raining.

'You'll get your book wet,' he said, and held out his hand to see what it was. 'So you've found it. And I can see from your face that you've discovered something else, haven't you? That's why I wanted you to try to find it yourself.'

'I bumped into my room-mate, Podorov. He said he met you once years ago.'

'Viktor Podorov, yes. I wonder what he told you. I'd forgotten all about him until Inspector Petersen gave me the list of all the mathematicians at the Institute. I wouldn't have recognised him anyway: I remember him as a rather troubled young man with a pointed beard, who thought he had a proof of Fermat's theorem. It was only much later that I remembered that I'd given a talk about Pythagorean numbers at that conference. I didn't want to mention it to

Inspector Petersen. I always felt a little guilty about Podorov. I heard that he tried to commit suicide when my student received the Fields Medal.'

'But it couldn't have been him, could it?' I asked. 'He was here in the library this evening.'

'No, I never really thought it was him, but I knew he was probably the only person who would see immediately how the series continued.'

'Yes,' I said, 'he remembered your lecture perfectly.'

We were standing beneath the semicircular awning at the entrance, getting splashed by the rain that was blowing in on gusts of wind.

'Let's make our way to the pub,' said Seldom.

I followed him, shielding the book from the rain. The pub seemed to be the only place open in all of Oxford. It was full of people talking in booming voices and laughing, with the exhilaration and slightly artificial cheerfulness that the English only seemed to achieve after a lot of beer. We sat at a table, the wood marked with wet rings.

'I'm sorry,' said the landlady from the bar, as if there was nothing she could do for us, 'you've missed last orders.'

'We can't stay here long,' said Seldom. 'I just wanted to know what you think, now that you know what the series is.'

'It's much simpler than anything a mathematician would have devised, isn't it? Maybe that's what's ingenious about it, but it's still a little disappointing. After all, it's just one, two, three, four, like the series of symmetrical figures you showed me the first day. But maybe it isn't a kind of puzzle, as we thought, but simply his way of enumerating the murders: first, second, third.'

'Yes,' said Seldom, 'that would be the worst-case scenario, because he could go on murdering indefinitely. But I still have hopes that the symbols are the challenge and that he'll stop if we show him that we know what the series is. Inspector Petersen just called me from his office. He's got an idea he thinks might be worth trying and apparently he has the psychologist's approval. He's changing tack regarding what appears in the papers: he's going to let the *Oxford Times* run an article about the third murder on its front page tomorrow, with a picture of the triangle and an interview in which he'll mention the first two symbols. The interview questions are going to be carefully prepared so as to make Petersen appear baffled by the murders and outwitted by the murderer. According to the psychologist, that'll provide our man with the sense of triumph he craves.

'The short note about the *tetraktys* that I wrote for Petersen will appear, with my name, in Thursday's edition, in the same section in which they published the chapter on serial murders from my book. That should be enough to show him that I *know* and can predict the symbol for the next murder. That keeps it on the level of the almost personal challenge that he seemed to lay down at the beginning.'

'But supposing it works,' I said, slightly taken aback, 'supposing, with luck, he reads your note in Thursday's paper and that, with a lot more luck, it stops him, how is Inspector Petersen going to catch him?'

'Petersen thinks it's only a matter of time. I think he's hoping that eventually a name will emerge from the list of those attending the concert. Anyway, he seems determined to try anything to avoid a fourth murder.'

'The interesting thing is that we've now got everything we need to predict the next step. I mean, we've got the three symbols, like in one of Frank Kalman's series, so we should be able to infer something about the fourth murder, to link the *tetraktys* . . . but to what? We still don't know anything about the link between the deaths and the symbols. But I've been thinking about what that doctor, Sanders, said, and I've found a recurring theme: in all three cases the victims were, in a way, living on borrowed time, longer than expected.'

'Yes, that's true,' said Seldom, 'I hadn't noticed . . .' His gaze became lost in the distance for a moment, as if he felt suddenly tired, overwhelmed by the constant ramifications of the case. 'I'm sorry,' he said, unsure of how long his mind had been elsewhere. 'I've got a bad feeling about this. I'd thought it a good idea to publicise the series. But perhaps there's too much time between tomorrow and Thursday.'

Chapter 18

I still have that Monday's copy of the *Oxford Times*, with the careful *mise en scène* for the benefit of a single phantom reader. As I now look at the slightly faded picture of the dead percussionist and the symbols, and reread the questions prepared for Inspector Petersen, I again sense, as if I were being touched by icy fingers, the shudder in Seldom's voice when he said perhaps there was too much time until Thursday. Above all, I understand, seeing them still clinging to the page, the horror he felt at the way conjectures in the real world acquired a mysterious life of their own. But on that particular bright morning I was free of premonitions and read about the case enthusiastically, and not without a little pride and no doubt some foolish vanity, knowing almost all of it already.

Lorna phoned me early. She sounded very excited – she too had just seen the article in the paper and she wanted us to have lunch together so that I could tell her absolutely *every-thing*. She couldn't forgive herself, or me, for having let her stay at home the previous evening while I was *there* at the concert. She hated me for it, but she'd escape from the hospital at lunchtime and meet me at the French café in Little Clarendon Street, so I shouldn't even think of planning anything with Emily for lunch. We met at the Café de Paris and laughed and chatted about the murders and ate crêpes with ham in the slightly irresponsible, invulnerable way of happy young lovers. I told Lorna what Inspector Petersen had said: the percussionist had had a very serious lung operation and his doctor was surprised that he hadn't died sooner.

'The same as with Ernest Clarck and Mrs Eagleton,' I said and waited for her reaction to my little theory. She thought for a moment.

'But that wasn't really Mrs Eagleton's case,' she said. 'I saw her at the hospital a couple of days before she died and she was delighted because tests had shown that her cancer was in remission. The doctor had told her she might live quite a few more years.'

'Well,' I said, as if that were a minor objection, 'that must have been a private conversation between her and her doctor, there was no way the murderer could have known.'

'So he chooses people who are living longer than expected? Is that what you mean?'

Her face darkened for a moment and she pointed to the television behind the bar, which she was facing. I turned and saw the smiling face of a little girl with curly hair on the screen and, beneath it, a telephone number and a request for all of the UK to call.

'Is that the little girl I saw at the hospital?' I asked Lorna. She nodded.

'She's top of the national transplant list now. She's got forty-eight hours at the most.'

'How's the father?' I asked. I still vividly remembered the frantic look in his eyes.

'I haven't seen him for a few days. I think he's had to go back to work.'

She put out her hand and intertwined her fingers in mine, as if to dispel the sudden dark cloud, and ordered another coffee. I drew a diagram on a napkin to show her the percussionist's location on the stage and asked if she knew of any way of inducing a respiratory arrest.

Lorna thought for a moment, stirring her coffee.

'I can only think of one way that would leave no trace: someone with sufficient strength could have climbed up the back and blocked the percussionist's mouth and nose with his hand. It's known as Burke's Death, after William Burke. Maybe you've seen his wax figure at Madame Tussaud's. He kept a lodging house in Edinburgh in the 1820s. He killed sixteen people and sold the bodies for dissection. It wouldn't take more than a few seconds to suffocate a person with very reduced lung capacity. I'd say that's how the murderer was killing the percussionist, when the spotlight swung back to him. He let go immediately, but the man was already in pulmonary and probably cardiac arrest too. What you all saw – the man holding his throat, as if he were being strangled by a ghost – was the typical reflex reaction of someone who can't breathe.'

'Another thing,' I said. 'Have you spoken to your friend the forensic pathologist again about Mr Clarck's post-

136

mortem? Inspector Petersen believes he has a different explanation.'

'No,' said Lorna, 'but he's asked me out to dinner several times. Do you think I should say yes and try to find out more?'

'No, no,' I said, laughing. 'I can live with the mystery.'

Lorna glanced at her watch.

'I've got to get back to the hospital,' she said, 'but you still haven't told me about the series. I hope it's nothing too difficult, I've forgotten all my maths.'

'No, the surprising thing is precisely how simple the solution is. The series is just one, two, three, four . . . in the notation used by the Pythagoreans.'

'The Pythagorean Brotherhood?' asked Lorna, as if this stirred a vague memory.

I nodded.

'I studied them briefly as part of my course, in History of Medicine. They believed in the transmigration of souls, didn't they? As far as I can remember they had a very cruel theory on the mentally retarded, which the Spartans and the doctors of Croton later put into practice. They valued intelligence highly and believed that the retarded were the reincarnation of people who had committed terrible sins in previous lives. They waited until they were fourteen, a critical age for those with Down's Syndrome, and they used the ones that survived as guinea pigs in their medical experiments. They were the first to try organ transplants. Pythagoras himself had a gold thigh. They were also the first vegetarians, but they weren't allowed to eat beans,' she said with a smile. 'And now I really must go.'

We said goodbye outside the café. I had to get back to

the Institute to write up the first report for my grant and I spent the next two hours going over papers and transcribing references. At a quarter to four I went downstairs, as I did every afternoon, to the Common Room, where the mathematicians gathered for coffee. The room was fuller than usual, as if nobody had stayed in their office that day, and I immediately heard the excited murmurs. Seeing them all together – shy, untidy, polite – I remembered Seldom's words. Yes, here they were, two and a half millennia later, queuing for their coffee in an orderly fashion, coins in hand, the arduous disciples of Pythagoras. There was a newspaper lying open on one of the tables and I assumed they were discussing the series of symbols. But I was wrong.

Emily joined me in the queue and said, with shining eyes, as if letting me in on a secret that still only few people knew: 'He's done it, apparently.' She said it as if she still couldn't believe it herself. When she saw my puzzled look, she added: 'Andrew Wiles! Haven't you heard? He's asked for two extra hours tomorrow at the Number Theory conference in Cambridge. He's proving the Shimura–Taniyama conjecture. If he gets to the end, he'll have proved Fermat's last theorem. A group of mathematicians are planning to go to Cambridge to be there tomorrow. It may be the most important day in the history of mathematics.'

Podorov arrived, looking sullen as usual. When he saw the queue he decided to sit and read the newspaper. I approached him, balancing a brimming cup of coffee and a muffin. Podorov looked up from the paper and glanced around contemptuously.

'So, have you signed up for the outing tomorrow? I can lend you my camera,' he said. 'They all want a little photo of Wiles's blackboard with the QED.'

'I'm not sure I'll be going,' I said.

'Why not? There's a free bus and Cambridge is a beautiful place too, in a very English way. Have you been?'

As he turned the page absently, his eyes alighted upon the long article about the murders and the series of symbols. He read the first two or three lines and, alarmed, wary, looked at me.

'You knew all about it yesterday, didn't you? How long have these murders been going on?' he asked.

I said that the first one occurred almost a month ago, but that the police had only now decided to reveal the symbols.

'And what is Seldom's part in all this?'

'The notes after each murder are addressed to him. The second message, with the symbol of the fish, appeared here, stuck to the revolving door at the entrance.'

'Ah, yes, I remember a small disturbance that morning. I saw the police, but I thought someone had broken a window.'

He went back to the newspaper and finished reading the article.

'But Seldom's name doesn't appear anywhere here.'

'The police don't want to reveal that the three messages have been addressed to him.'

He looked at me again but his expression had changed: he now seemed amused.

'So someone is playing cat and mouse with the great Seldom. Perhaps there is divine justice after all. Dispensed by a mathematician god, of course,' he said mysteriously. 'What do you imagine the fourth murder will be like?' he asked. 'A death in keeping with the ancient solemnity of the *tetraktys*?' He looked around as if searching for inspiration. 'I seem to remember that Seldom liked bowling, at least at one time,' he said. 'The game wasn't very well known in Russia then. In his lecture, he compared the points of the *tetraktys* to the layout of the pins at the start of a game. And there's a shot where you knock down all ten pins on the first ball.'

'Strike,' I said.

'Yes, exactly. Isn't that a magnificent word?' And he repeated it in his strong Russian accent, smiling strangely, as if he was picturing an implacable ball and heads rolling. 'Strike!'

Chapter 19

By five o'clock I'd finished the first draft of my report. Before leaving the office I checked my e-mail again. There was a short message from Seldom asking me to meet him at Merton after his seminar, if I was free. I'd have to hurry to get there on time. I climbed the small staircase that led to the classrooms and, peering through the glass door, saw him discussing a problem on the blackboard with two students who had stayed behind.

The students left and he motioned for me to enter. While he put away his notes, he pointed to a circle drawn on the board and said:

'We were discussing Nicholas of Cusa's geometrical metaphor – the truth as a circumference and human attempts to approach it as a series of inscribed polygons, with more and more sides, coming close in the end to a circular form. It's an optimistic metaphor, because successive stages enable one to sense the final figure. There is, however, another possibility, one that my students still aren't aware of and which is much more discouraging.' Beside the circle he quickly drew an irregular figure with numerous points and clefts. 'Suppose for a moment that the truth was the shape, say, of an island like Britain, with a very irregular coastline, with endless projections and inlets. This time, when you try to approximate the figure by means of polygons, you encounter Mandelbrot's paradox. The edge remains elusive, breaking up at each new attempt into ever more projections and inlets, and human efforts to determine it simply never arrive at a final figure. Similarly, the truth may not yield to the series of human approximations. What does this remind you of?'

'Gödel's theorem? The polygons would be systems with more and more axioms, but a part of the truth is always beyond reach.'

'Perhaps, in a sense. But it's also like this case, and Wittgenstein's and Frankie's conclusion: the known terms of a series, any number of terms, are always insufficient. How can one know a priori with which of these two figures we're dealing? You know,' he said suddenly, 'my father had a big library, with a bookcase in the middle where he kept the books I wasn't allowed to read, a bookcase with a door that locked. When he opened it, all I could ever see was an engraving he'd stuck inside, of a man touching the ground with one hand and holding his other arm up in the air. Under the picture there was a caption in a language I didn't know, which I eventually found out was German. I also later discovered a book that I thought miraculous: a bilingual dictionary my father used

142

when he was teaching his classes. I deciphered the words one by one. The sentence was simple and mysterious: "Man is no more than the series of his actions." I had a child's absolute faith in the words and I started to see people as temporary, incomplete figures; figures in draft form, ever elusive. If a man is no more than the series of his actions, I realised, then he can't be defined before his death: a single action, his last, could wipe out his previous existence, contradict his entire life. And, above all, it was precisely the series of my actions that I most feared. Man was no more than what I most feared.'

He showed me his hands, which were covered in chalk dust. He must have touched his face inadvertently because there was also a comical white mark on his forehead.

'I'll be back in a minute – I'm just going to wash my hands,' he said. 'If you go downstairs you'll find the cafeteria. Would you get me a large coffee, please? Without sugar.'

I ordered two coffees. Seldom reappeared just in time to carry his own cup to a table set slightly apart from the rest, with a view of the gardens. Through the open door of the cafeteria we could see the continuous stream of tourists entering the college and heading for the quads.

'I had a chat with Inspector Petersen this morning,' said Seldom. 'He told me about their dilemma over the counting yesterday evening. On one hand they knew the exact number of people who entered the gardens of the palace from the ticket stubs collected as they arrived, and on the other they knew the number of seats occupied. The person in charge of seating is particularly meticulous and assured them that he had added only the chairs that were strictly needed. Now here's the strange thing: when they finished the count it turned out that there were more people than seats. Three people didn't use their seats.'

Seldom looked at me as if expecting me to find the explanation immediately. I pondered for a moment, slightly embarrassed.

'I thought it wasn't done in England to sneak into concerts without paying,' I said.

Seldom laughed frankly.

'Not to charity concerts anyway. Oh, don't think about it any more; it really is very silly. Petersen was just teasing me. He was in a good mood for once today. The three extra people were disabled, in wheelchairs. Petersen was delighted with his counting. In the list drawn up by his assistants there was nobody missing and nobody extra. For the first time he thinks he's narrowed down the search: instead of the five hundred thousand people in Oxfordshire, now he only has to concern himself with the eight hundred who attended the concert. And he thinks he'll quickly be able to narrow it down even further.'

'The three people in wheelchairs,' I said.

Seldom smiled.

'Yes, in theory the three wheelchair users as well as a group of children with Down's Syndrome from a special school, and several very elderly ladies – the most likely – could all have been potential victims.'

'Do you think the deciding factor in his choice of victim is age?'

'I know you've got another theory: that he chooses people who are living on borrowed time, living longer than expected. Yes, in that case age would not be an excluding factor.'

'Did Petersen tell you anything else about the death last night? Does he have the results of the post-mortem?'

'Yes. He wanted to rule out the possibility that the percussionist ingested something before the concert which might have caused the respiratory arrest. And sure enough, they found nothing like that. Nor were there any signs of violence, no marks on his neck. Petersen thinks the man was attacked by someone who was familiar with the music: he chose the longest section without percussion. That meant he could be sure the percussionist would be out of the spotlight. Petersen has also ruled out it being another member of the orchestra. The only answer, given the percussionist's location at the back of the stage and the absence of marks on his neck, is that someone climbed up the back and . . .'

'Covered his mouth and nose.'

Seldom looked at me, surprised.

'That's what Lorna thought,' I told him.

He nodded.

'Yes, I should have guessed: Lorna knows all there is to know about crime. The pathologist says that the shock of being attacked could in itself have triggered the respiratory arrest, before the percussionist even tried to struggle. Someone climbed up the back and attacked him in the darkness – that seems like the only reasonable explanation. But that wasn't what we saw.'

'You surely not tending towards the ghost hypothesis?' I said

To my surprise, Seldom seemed to give my question serious consideration. He nodded slowly.

'Yes,' he said, 'of the two alternatives, for now, I prefer the hypothesis of the ghost.'

He drank some coffee and looked at me again.

'You shouldn't let your eagerness to find an explanation interfere with your memory of events. Actually, I asked you to meet me because I wanted you to have a look at this.'

He opened his briefcase and took out an envelope.

'Petersen showed me these photographs when I went to his office today. I asked if I could keep them till tomorrow so I could look at them carefully. I particularly wanted you to see them: they're the photos of the crime scene at Mrs Eagleton's – the first murder, the start of everything. The inspector's returned to the original question: how is the circle in the first note linked to Mrs Eagleton? As you know, I think you saw something else there, something you still haven't realised is important, but which is stored in a recess of your memory. I thought the photos might help you remember. It's all here again.' He held out the envelope. 'The sitting room, the cuckoo clock, the chaise longue, the Scrabble board. We know that in that first murder *he made a mistake*. That should tell us something more . . .' Seldom was distracted for a moment. He looked round at the other tables and the corridor. Suddenly his face hardened as if he'd seen something alarming.

'Someone's just left something in my pigeonhole,' he said. 'It's odd because the postman's already been this morning. I hope Detective Sergeant Sacks is still around. Wait here a minute, I'm going to have a look.'

I swivelled in my chair and saw that from where Seldom was sitting he could just see the last column of wooden pigeonholes on the wall. So that was where he'd received the first note. I was struck by the fact that the correspondence of all the members of the college was so openly on display in the corridor. The pigeonholes at the Mathematical Institute were equally unprotected. When Seldom came back he was looking at something inside an envelope, with a big smile on his face as if he'd just had unexpected good news.

'Do you remember the magician I mentioned, René Lavand? He's in Oxford today and tomorrow. I've got tickets here for this evening. It has to be tonight because I'll be in Cambridge tomorrow. Are you coming on our mathematicians' outing?'

'No, I don't think so,' I said. 'It's Lorna's day off tomorrow.'

Seldom raised his eyebrows slightly.

'The solution to the most important problem in the history of mathematics versus a beautiful woman. The girl still wins, I suppose.'

'But I would very much like to see the magician's show this evening.'

'Of course, of course,' said Seldom, unusually vehement. 'You absolutely must see it. It starts at nine. And now,' he said, as if he were giving me a homework assignment, 'go home and look carefully at the photographs.'

Chapter 20

When I got back to my room I prepared a pot of coffee, made the bed and laid out the photographs from the envelope on the bedcover. As I looked at them I remembered the words, like a quiet axiom of a figurative painter: there is always less reality in a photo than can be captured in a painting. Indeed, something seemed to have been irretrievably lost from the fragmented picture made up of flawlessly sharp images that I composed on the bed.

I tried putting the photographs in a different order, shifting a few. *Something that I had seen.* I tried again, setting out the photographs in accordance with what I remembered seeing when we entered Mrs Eagleton's sitting room. Something that I had seen but Seldom hadn't. Why only me, why couldn't he have seen it too? *Because you'd had no warning*, Seldom had said. Perhaps it was like one of those three-dimensional computer-generated images that had become so fashionable, quite invisible to an attentive eye, only appearing gradually, fleetingly, when you relaxed your attention. The first thing I'd seen was Seldom, walking quickly towards me up the gravel path. There was no photo of him here, but I clearly recalled our conversation at the front door and the moment when he asked me about Mrs Eagleton. I'd pointed out the electric wheelchair in the hall, so he too had seen the chair. He'd turned the door handle, the door had opened silently and we'd entered the sitting room together. After that everything was more confused. I could remember the sound of the pendulum, though I wasn't sure if I'd glanced at the clock.

Anyway, the photograph showing the door from the inside, the coat stand and the clock should come first in the sequence. That image, I thought, would also have been the last thing the murderer saw as he left. I put the photograph down and wondered which should come next. Had I seen anything else before we found Mrs Eagleton? I'd automatically looked for her in the same flowery armchair that she'd greeted me from the first day. I picked up a photo of the two little armchairs standing on the diamond-patterned rug. You could just see the handles of her wheelchair behind one of them. Had I noticed the wheelchair when I was there? I couldn't say for sure. It was exasperating: suddenly everything was eluding me.

The only focus in my memory was Mrs Eagleton's body lying on the chaise longue and her open eyes, as if this one image radiated a light so intense that it left everything else in shadow. But, as we went closer, I had seen the Scrabble board and the two letter racks on her side. One of the photos had frozen the position of the board on the little table. It had been taken from very close up and you just could make out all the words. Seldom and I had already discussed the words on the board and neither of us thought they revealed anything interesting, or that they were linked in any way with the symbol in the note. Inspector Petersen hadn't thought them important either. We agreed that the symbol had been chosen before the murder, not by an inspiration of the moment. I peered anyway at the photos of the letter racks. I was sure I hadn't seen *this*: there was only one letter, an A, on one rack, and only two, an R and an O, on the other. Mrs Eagleton must have played to the end – until she'd used up all the letters in the bag – before falling asleep. I tried for a while to think of words in English that could be formed on the board with those last remaining letters, but there didn't seem to be any, and besides, I thought, if there had been, Mrs Eagleton would surely have found them. Why hadn't I noticed the letter racks before? I tried to remember their position on the table. They were at one corner, nearest to where Seldom had stood holding the pillow. Perhaps, I thought, I had to find precisely what I *hadn't* seen. I scanned the photos again, to see if I could detect any details I might have missed, until I came to the last one, the still terrifying image of Mrs Eagleton's lifeless face. I couldn't find anything I hadn't noticed before. So it must be those three things: the letter racks, the clock in the hall, and the wheelchair.

The wheelchair . . . Did that explain the symbol? A triangle for the percussionist, the fish tank for Clark, and for Mrs Eagleton, the circle – the wheel of her wheelchair perhaps. *Or the O of the word 'omertà'*, Seldom had said.

150

Yes, the circle could still be almost anything. But, interestingly, there was a letter O on one of the letter racks. Or perhaps it wasn't interesting at all, but just a silly coincidence? Perhaps Seldom had seen the O on the letter rack, and that was why he'd thought of the word '*omertà*'. Seldom had said something else, the day we went to the Covered Market, that he was confident I would see something *because I wasn't English*. But what was a non-English way of seeing?

I was startled by the sound of someone trying to push an envelope under my door. I opened it and found Beth straightening up quickly, red-faced. She was holding several more envelopes.

'I thought you were out,' she said. 'Or I would have knocked.'

I invited her in and picked up the envelope. Inside, there was a card with an illustration from *Alice through the Looking Glass* and the words 'Non-wedding Invitation' in embossed letters.

I smiled at her, intrigued.

'The thing is, we can't get married yet,' said Beth. 'Michael's divorce could take ages. But we still want to have a celebration.' She caught sight of the photos lying all over the bed. 'Photos of your family?'

'No, I don't have any family in the usual sense. They're the photos the police took the day of Mrs Eagleton's murder.'

Beth, I reflected, was definitely English and her gaze was as representative as any other. And she was the last person to have seen Mrs Eagleton alive, so she might notice if anything looked different. I motioned for her to approach but she hesitated, a look of horror on her face. At last she took a couple of steps forwards and glanced at the photographs quickly, as if afraid to look more closely.

'Why have they given you these after all this time? What do you think they can still find out from them?'

'They want to find the link between Mrs Eagleton and the first symbol. Perhaps if you look at them now, you'll see something else – something missing or moved.'

'But I've already told Inspector Petersen: I can't remember exactly where every single thing was when I left the house. When I came downstairs I saw that she was asleep, so I left as quietly as I could, without even glancing at her again. I've already been over this once. That afternoon, when Uncle Arthur came to the theatre to tell me what had happened, they were waiting for me in the sitting room, with the body still there.'

As if determined to overcome her terror, she picked up the photograph of Mrs Eagleton stretched out on the chaise longue. 'All I could tell them,' she said, touching the photo with her finger, 'was that the blanket for her legs was missing. She never lay down without a blanket over her legs, not even on the warmest days. She didn't want anyone to see her scars. We searched for the blanket all over the house that day but it never turned up.'

'It's true,' I said, amazed that we hadn't noticed. 'I never saw her without that blanket. Why would the murderer have wanted to expose her scars? Or perhaps he took the blanket as a souvenir? Maybe he's kept mementoes of the other two murders as well.'

'I don't know, I don't want to have to think about any

of this again,' Beth said, heading towards the door. 'It's been a nightmare. I wish it was all over. When we saw Benito die in the middle of the concert and Inspector Petersen appeared on the stage, I thought I would die myself there and then. All I could think was that he was somehow going to lay the blame on me again.'

'No, he immediately ruled out anyone from the orchestra. It had to be someone who climbed up and attacked him from behind.'

'Well, whatever he thinks,' said Beth, shaking her head, 'I just hope they catch him soon and it'll all be over.' Her hand on the door handle, she turned to say: 'Your girlfriend's welcome to come to the party too, of course. She's the one you play tennis with, isn't she?'

Once Beth had gone, I slowly put the photographs back in the envelope. The invitation lay on the bed. The picture was actually of the un-birthday party or, more precisely, just one of the three hundred and sixty-four un-birthday parties that Lewis Carroll teases us with. The logician in him knew that what remains outside each statement is always overwhelmingly larger.

The blanket was a small, exasperating alarm signal. How much more was there in each murder that we hadn't been able to see? Perhaps that was what Seldom was hoping for from me: that I should picture what wasn't there but that we should have seen.

Still thinking about Beth, I searched a drawer for a change of clothes before taking a shower. The telephone rang: it was Lorna. She was free that evening after all. I asked if she'd like to come to the magic show.

'Of course I would,' she said. 'I don't intend to miss any more of your outings. But now that I'm going with you, I'm sure we'll see nothing but silly rabbits pulled out of hats.'

Chapter 21

When we arrived at the theatre there were no more seats available in the front rows, so Seldom kindly offered Lorna his while he sat further back. The stage was in darkness, but you could make out a table on which stood a large glass of water, and a high-backed armchair facing the audience. Just behind, there were a dozen empty chairs set out in a semicircle around the table. We entered the auditorium a few minutes after the start of the show and the lights were going down as we took our seats. The theatre was in darkness for what seemed like only a fraction of a second before a spotlight was directed at the stage and the magician appeared, sitting in the armchair, as if he'd been there all along. He peered into the audience, holding his hand above his eyes like a visor.

'Light! More light!' he demanded. He stood up and

walked round the table to the edge of the stage, hand still shielding his eyes, scanning the audience.

A cruel surgical light illuminated his bent figure. Only then did I notice with surprise that he had only one arm. His right arm was missing, amputated cleanly at the shoulder, as if he had never had one. He raised his left arm again imperiously.

'More light!' he demanded again. 'I want you to see everything, so that no one can say, "It was an effect of smoke and shadow." Even if it means you can see my wrinkles. My seven folds of wrinkles. Yes, I'm very old, aren't I? Almost *unbelievably* old. And yet, I was once a child of eight, I once had two hands, like all of you, and I wanted to learn magic. "No, don't teach me tricks," I'd say to my teacher. Because I wanted to be a magician, I didn't want to learn tricks. But my teacher, who was almost as old as I am now, said: "The first step is knowing the tricks."'

The magician spread his fingers and held them like a fan in front of his face. 'I can tell you, because it no longer matters, that my fingers were extremely quick and agile. I had a natural gift and very soon I was travelling all over my country– the little conjuror, almost a circus freak. But at the age of ten I had an accident. Or maybe it wasn't an accident. When I woke up I was in a hospital bed and I only had my left arm. I, who wanted to be a magician. I, who was right-handed. But my old teacher was there and, while my parents wept, all he said was: "This is the second step. Perhaps you'll be a magician some day." My teacher died, and nobody ever told me what the third step was. Since then, every time I go on stage I wonder if that day has come. Perhaps this is something that only you, the audience, can say. That's why I always call for more light, and I ask you to come up on stage, to come and see. This way.' One by one he made half of the people in the front row come up on stage and sit in the chairs all around him. 'Closer, closer. I want you to watch my hand, not to be taken by surprise, because remember, I don't want to perform tricks here today.'

He held out his bare hand over the table, holding something small and white between thumb and forefinger. I couldn't see what it was from where we were sitting.

'I come from a country they used to call the Bread Basket of the World. "Don't leave, son," my mother would say. "You'll never lack bread here." I left, but I always have this little piece of bread with me.' He held it out again between two fingers, swivelling so that we could all see, before placing it carefully on the table. He pressed down with his palm in a circular movement, as if to knead it. 'How strange these trails of breadcrumbs are. Birds remove them at night so that we cannot follow the trails back. "Come back, son," my mother would say, "you'll never lack bread here." But I couldn't go back. How strange these trails of breadcrumbs are! Trails that you can follow away but not back.' His hand was circling hypnotically above the table. 'That's why I didn't use up all my breadcrumbs on the way. And wherever I go, I always have with me . . .' – he held up his hand and we saw that he was holding a small perfectly formed bread roll, the pointed ends protruding from his fist – '. . . a piece of bread.'

He turned and held out the roll to the first person in the semicircle.

157

'Don't be afraid. Have some.' The hand, like the hand of a clock, moved to the second person and opened again to reveal a rounded, intact end. 'You can take a larger piece. Come, try some.' He turned to each of the people sitting on the chairs, until they had all had a piece of bread roll.

'Yes,' he said thoughtfully when he had finished. He opened out his hand and there was the little bread roll, still intact. He straightened out his very long fingers before slowly closing his fist again. When he opened it, all that remained was the little piece of bread, which he held up between thumb and forefinger to show us. 'You mustn't use up all your breadcrumbs on the way.'

He rose to receive the applause and stood at the edge of the stage dismissing the people who had occupied the chairs. Lorna and I were in the second group to go up on stage. I could now see him from the side with his hooked nose, very black moustache, that looked dyed, and lank grey hair clinging to his skull. But I was struck above all by his large, bony hand with liver spots on the back. He slipped it around the glass and took a sip of water before continuing.

'I like to call this part of the show "Slowification",' he said. He took a pack of cards from his pocket and began shuffling it fantastically fast with his only hand. 'Tricks cannot be repeated, my teacher used to say. But I didn't want to perform tricks, I wanted to perform magic. Can one repeat an act of magic? Only six cards,' he said, taking them one by one from the pack. 'Three red, three black. Red and black. The black of night, the red of life. Can anyone control colours? Can anyone impose an order on them?' With a flick of the thumb, he tossed the cards down

158

on the table, one after another, facing up. 'Red, black, red, black, red, black.' The cards lay in a row, red and black alternating.

'And now, watch my hand. I want to do it very slowly.' He moved his hand forward to pick up the cards in the order in which they lay. 'Can anyone impose an order on them?' he said again and flung them back down on the table with the same flick of the thumb. 'Red, red, red, black, black, black. It could not be done any slower,' he said, gathering up the cards. 'Or perhaps ... it *could*.' Again, he tossed down the cards with the colours alternating, letting them fall slowly. 'Red, black, red, black, red, black.' He turned towards us so that we could see exactly what he was doing. He inched his hand forward, as slowly as a crab, touching the first card with the tips of his fingers. He picked the cards up extremely gently and, when he threw them back down on the table, the colours had come together once more. 'Red, red, red, black, black, black.'

'But this young man,' he said, suddenly turning his gaze upon me, 'remains sceptical. Perhaps he's read some manual of magic and thinks the trick is in the way I pick up the cards, or in a glide effect. Yes, that's how he'd do it. That's how I did it myself when I had two hands. But now I've only got one. And perhaps some day I won't have any.' He flung the cards down on the table one by one. 'Red, black, red, black, red, black.' Looking at me again, he commanded: 'Gather them up. And now, without letting me touch them, turn them over one by one.' I obeyed, and, as I turned them over, the cards seemed to submit to his will. 'Red, red, red, black, black, black.'

When we returned to our seats, while the audience was still applauding, I realised why Seldom had insisted I should see the show. Each of the tricks that followed was, like the first ones, extraordinarily simple and also extraordinarily pure, as if the old man had truly reached a golden moment in which he no longer needed his hands. And it seemed to amuse him to break the rules of his trade, one by one. He repeated tricks, he had people sitting behind him during the entire show, he revealed techniques with which other magicians throughout the ages had attempted the same effects. At one point I turned round and saw Seldom completely enthralled, happily lost in admiration, like a child who never tires of seeing the same marvel over and over. I recalled how serious he was when he said that he preferred the ghost hypothesis for the third murder, and I wondered if he really believed such things. But it was difficult not to give in to the magician: the skill of each trick lay in its essential simplicity and the only explanation always seemed to be an impossible one. There was no interval and all too suddenly he announced his final trick.

'You must have wondered,' he said, 'why I have such a large glass of water when all I've taken is one small sip. There's still enough water here for a fish to swim about in.' He brought out a red silk handkerchief and slowly wiped the glass. 'Perhaps,' he said, 'if we clean the glass well and imagine little coloured pebbles, perhaps, as in the cage in Prévert's poem, we'll catch a fish.' When he withdrew the handkerchief, there was a goldfish swimming around inside the glass and little coloured pebbles at the bottom.

'As you know, we magicians have been cruelly persecuted through the ages, ever since the fire in which the

Pythagorean magicians, our most ancient forefathers, perished. Yes, mathematics and magic have common roots, and for a long time they guarded the same secret. We were most savagely persecuted after the struggle between Peter and Simon Magus, when the Christians officially banned magic. They feared that someone else might be able to multiply the loaves and fishes. It was then that magicians devised what remains today their survival strategy: they wrote manuals explaining the most obvious tricks and circulated them among the people, and they used silly boxes and mirrors in their shows. They gradually convinced everyone that there was a trick behind every act of magic. They became armchair magicians, indistinguishable from vulgar conjurors, and in that way were able to continue in secret, doing their own multiplying of loaves and fishes under their persecutors' very noses.

'Yes, the most subtle and enduring trick was to convince everyone that magic does not exist. I myself just used this handkerchief. But for true magicians, the handkerchief doesn't conceal a trick, but a much more ancient secret. So remember,' he said with a mischievous smile, 'always remember: magic does not exist.' He clicked his fingers and another goldfish jumped into the water. 'Magic does not exist.' He clicked his fingers again and a third fish jumped into the glass. He covered the glass with the handkerchief and, when he removed it, there remained neither pebbles nor fish nor glass. 'Magic . . . does not exist.'

Chapter 22

We were in the Eagle and Child, and Seldom and Lorna were teasing me for taking so long to finish my beer.

'It *could not be drunk any slower . . . or perhaps it could*,' said Lorna imitating the magician's deep, slightly rasping voice.

We had gone to see Lavand in his dressing room briefly after the show and Seldom had tried, unsuccessfully, to persuade him to come with us to the pub. 'Ah yes, our young sceptic,' the magician had said absently when Seldom introduced me and then, when he found out I, like him, was Argentinian, he said in Spanish that sounded as if he hadn't used it in a long time, 'Magic is safe thanks to the sceptics.' He was very tired, he told us, reverting to English. He was making his shows shorter and shorter but he couldn't fool his old bones. 'We must talk again before I leave,' he said to Seldom at the door. 'I hope you find something about what you asked me in the book I lent you.'

'What did you ask the magician about? What book did he mean?' enquired Lorna confidently. The beer seemed to have a strange effect on her of recovered camaraderie, which I'd noticed in the way she smiled when she and Seldom clinked glasses, and I wondered again how far their friendship had gone.

'I told him about the death of the percussionist,' said Seldom. 'And I asked him about an idea that I considered at one point, when I remembered how Mrs Crafford died.'

'Ah, yes,' said Lorna enthusiastically, 'the case of the telepath.'

'It was one of Inspector Petersen's most famous cases,' said Seldom, addressing me. 'The death of Mrs Crafford, a very wealthy old lady who ran the local spiritualist circle. The qualifying rounds of the World Chess Championship were being held here in Oxford at the time. A well-known Indian telepath was in town and Mr and Mrs Crafford held a soirée at their mansion to try an experiment in remote telepathy. The Craffords' house was in Summertown, close to where you live. The telepath was to be across town, at Folly Bridge. The distance was supposedly some sort of record. Mrs Crafford had gladly volunteered to be the first test subject. With great ceremony, the Indian telepath asked her to sit in the middle of the sitting room, placed a kind of skullcap on her head and left the house, heading for the bridge. At the appointed time, they turned out the lights. The cap was fluorescent and glowed in the dark, and the people in the audience could see a ghostly aura around Mrs Crafford's face. After thirty seconds they suddenly heard a terrible scream, followed by a long sizzling sound like eggs frying. When Mr Crafford switched the lights back on they found the old lady dead in her chair, with her skull burnt, as if she'd been struck by lightning.

'The poor telepath was arrested as a preventative measure, until he managed to explain that the cap was totally harmless, simply a piece of cloth covered in fluorescent paint designed purely for effect. The man was as baffled as everyone else: he'd performed his remote telepathy show in many countries, under all kinds of atmospheric conditions, and that day had been particularly clear and sunny. Inspector Petersen of course immediately turned his suspicions on Mr Crafford. It was common knowledge that he was having an affair with a much younger woman, but there seemed to be very little else to implicate him. And it was difficult to imagine *how* he could have done it. Petersen based his case against him on a single fact: that day Mrs Crafford had been wearing what she called her "dress wig", which had wire mesh on the inside. Everyone had seen Mr Crafford kiss his wife affectionately just before the lights were turned out. Inspector Petersen claimed that at that moment Crafford had connected a wire to the wig to electrocute her, which he later removed when he pretended to go to her aid. It wasn't impossible, but as was shown later at the trial, it would have been rather difficult.

'Crafford's lawyer, on the other hand, had a simple and, in its way, brilliant explanation. If you look at a map of the city, halfway between Folly Bridge and Summertown you find the Playhouse, where the chess championship was being held. At the time of Mrs Crafford's death, around a

164

hundred chess players were concentrating furiously on their chessboards. The defence maintained that the mental energy liberated by the telepath had suddenly been boosted by all the energy from the players as it passed through the theatre, hitting Summertown like a whirlwind. And that would explain how what was at first merely a harmless brain wave ended up striking Mrs Crafford like a bolt of lightning. Crafford's trial divided Oxford into two camps. The defence called to the stand an army of mentalists and supposed experts on the paranormal who, predictably, backed up the lawyer's theory with all kinds of ridiculous explanations, couched in the usual pseudo-scientific jargon. The odd thing was that the more crazy the theory, the more prepared the jury – and the entire town – seemed to be to believe it.

'At that time I was just starting my work on the aesthetics of reasoning and I was fascinated by the strength of conviction that an attractive idea could generate. True, one could argue that the jury was probably made up of people with no scientific training, people more apt to trust horoscopes, the *I Ching* and tarot cards than to doubt parapsychologists and telepaths. But the interesting thing is that the entire city embraced the idea and wanted to believe it, not due to an attack of irrationality but for supposedly scientific reasons. It was in a way a battle within the rational, and the theory of the chess players was simply more seductive, more clearly defined, more pregnant, as painters would say, than the theory of the wire mesh in the wig.

'But then, just as everything seemed to be going Crafford's way, the *Oxford Times* printed a letter from a reader, a certain Lorna Craig, a girl who was a huge fan of crime novels,' said Seldom, indicating Lorna with his glass. They smiled, as if sharing an old joke. 'The letter simply pointed out that in an old edition of *Ellery Queen's Mystery Magazine* there was a story about a similar death by remote telepathy, the only difference being that the brain wave went through a football stadium during a penalty shot instead of through a room full of chess players. The funny thing was that in the story the theory of the brainstorm, now put forward by Crafford's lawyer, was taken to be true and to be the solution to the mystery. But how fickle is human nature: as soon as people found out that Crafford might have copied the idea, they all turned against him. The lawyer tried to persuade the jury that Crafford wasn't much of a reader and was unlikely to know the story, but it was no use. The idea, by dint of repetition, had lost some of its attraction and now sounded ridiculous, like something that only a writer could have thought up. The jury, a jury of fallible men, as Kant would say, found Crafford guilty even though no other proof against him had been found. Let us say this: the only piece of evidence presented during the entire trial was a fantastical story that poor Crafford had never even read.'

'*Poor* Crafford fried his wife!' exclaimed Lorna.

'As you can see,' laughed Seldom, 'some people were totally convinced of his guilt and didn't need proof. Anyway, I remembered the case the night of the concert. If you recall, the percussionist suffocated just as the music reached the climax. Well, I asked Lavand about the kind of effects that can be created from a distance and he lent me a book on hypnotism. I haven't had time to look at it yet.'

166

A waitress came to take our order. Lorna said I should have fish and chips, and then got up to go to the ladies. Once Seldom had ordered and the waitress had left, I returned the envelope containing the photographs to him.

'Were you able to *remember* anything?' he asked. When he saw my doubtful look, he said: 'It's difficult, isn't it? Going back to the beginning as if one knew nothing. Emptying one's mind of all that came afterwards. Did you see anything that you hadn't noticed before?'

'Only this: when we found Mrs Eagleton's body, she didn't have a blanket over her legs,' I said.

Seldom leaned back in his chair and stroked his chin.

'That . . . could be interesting,' he said. 'Yes, now that you mention it, I remember clearly, she always had a tartan blanket over her legs. When she was going out, at least.'

'Beth is sure that her grandmother still had the blanket when she came downstairs at two. The police searched the house for it later but couldn't find it. Inspector Petersen didn't mention any of this to us,' I said a little resentfully.

'Well,' said Seldom, gently mocking, 'he is the police inspector in charge of the case. Perhaps he doesn't feel the need to report every single detail to us.'

I laughed.

'But we know more than he does,' I said.

'Only in the sense that we're familiar with Pythagoras's theorem.'

His face darkened, as if suddenly reminded of his worst fears. He leaned towards me and said confidentially:

'His daughter told me he has trouble sleeping at night. She's found him awake in the early hours several times, trying to read books on mathematics. He called me again this morning. I think he's worried, like me, that Thursday will be too late.'

'But Thursday is only the day after tomorrow,' I said.

'*Pasado mañana*,' said Seldom. 'The day after tomorrow. The thing is, tomorrow is no ordinary day. That was why Petersen called. He wants to send some of his men to Cambridge.'

'What's happening tomorrow in Cambridge?' Lorna was back, carrying our beers.

'I have a feeling it's all because of the book I lent Petersen, giving a rather fanciful account of the story of Fermat's theorem. It's the most ancient unsolved problem in mathematics,' he said to Lorna. 'Mathematicians have been struggling with it for over three hundred years and, tomorrow in Cambridge, they may manage to prove it for the first time. The book traces the origin of the conjecture on Pythagorean triples, one of the secrets of the earliest years of the sect, before the fire when, as Lavand said, magic and mathematics were still closely linked. The Pythagoreans believed that numerical properties and relationships represented the secret number of a deity which should be kept secret within the sect. They could disseminate theorems, for use in daily life, but never their proofs, just as magicians swear not to reveal their tricks. Members of the sect broke this rule on pain of death.

'The book I lent Inspector Petersen claims that Fermat himself belonged to a more recent but no less strict sect than the Pythagoreans. He announced in his famous note in the margin to Diophantus's *Arithmetica* that he had proof of his conjecture but, after his death, neither that nor any of his other proofs were found among his papers.

I expect what alarmed Petersen was the fact that there are several strange deaths linked with the story of the theorem. A lot of people have died, of course, over the three hundred years, including those who came close to finding a proof of the theorem. But the book's author is shrewd and he manages to make some of the deaths seem truly suspicious – Taniyama's suicide in the late fifties, for instance, with the strange note he left for his fiancée.'

'In that case the murders would be . . .'

'A warning,' said Seldom. 'A warning to the world of mathematicians. As I told Petersen, I think the conspiracy set out in the book is probably a load of ingenious nonsense. But there is something that worries me: Andrew Wiles has worked in absolute secret for the past seven years. Nobody has a clue as to what his proof will be. He has never allowed me to look at any of his papers. If something should happen to him before his presentation and those papers disappeared, another three hundred years might pass before anyone repeated the proof. That's why, quite apart from what I think, it's not a bad idea for Petersen to send some of his men to Cambridge. If anything happened to Andrew,' he said, and his face darkened again, 'I'd never forgive myself.'

Chapter 23

On Wednesday 23 June I woke around midday. The heavenly smells of coffee and freshly made waffles were coming from Lorna's tiny kitchen. Her cat, Sir Thomas, had managed to drag part of the bedspread on to the floor and he was now curled up on it at the foot of the bed. I walked around him and went to the kitchen to kiss Lorna. The paper was open on the table and I glanced through it while Lorna poured the coffee. A series of murders with mysterious symbols, said the *Oxford Times* with undisguised local pride, had become the lead story in the main London papers. They reproduced on their front page some of the headlines from the previous day's national papers. But that was all, there had obviously been no new developments in the case.

I searched the inside pages for news of the seminar in Cambridge. All I found was a brief item entitled

'Mathematicians' Moby Dick', including the long list of failed attempts to prove Fermat's theorem over the years. The article mentioned that bets were being laid in Oxbridge on the outcome of the last of the afternoon's three lectures and the odds at the moment were still six-to-one against Wiles.

Lorna had booked a tennis court for one o'clock. We stopped off at Cunliffe Close to collect my racket and then played for a long time without being interrupted, concentrating only on the ball going back and forth over the net, in that small rectangle out of time. As we left the courts I saw on the clubhouse clock that it was almost three and I asked Lorna if we could make a quick stop at the Institute on the way back. The building was deserted and I had to switch on lights as I went upstairs. In the computer room, which was empty too, I checked my e-mail. There was the short message that was being spread like a password to mathematicians all over the world: *Wiles had done it*! There were no details about the final exposition. All it said was that his proof had convinced the experts and that, once written up, it might be up to two hundred pages long.

'Good news?' asked Lorna as I got back in the car.

I told her, and in my admiring tone she must have caught the strange contradictory pride I felt in mathematicians.

'Perhaps you would rather have been there this afternoon,' she said and then, laughing: 'What can I do to make it up to you?'

We spent the rest of the afternoon making love like a pair of happy rabbits. At seven, as it was getting dark, we were lying side by side in exhausted silence when the telephone rang. Lorna leaned across me to answer it. A look of alarm appeared on her face, and then horrified sorrow. She indicated that I should turn on the television and, with the phone wedged between shoulder and chin, she started dressing.

'There's been an accident on the way into Oxford, at a spot they call the "blind triangle". A bus drove over the side of the bridge and down the bank. They're expecting several ambulances with the injured at the Radcliffe – they need me in the X-ray department.'

I changed channels until I found the local news. A female reporter was talking as she moved closer to the shattered barrier of the bridge. I pressed buttons on the remote but couldn't get any sound.

'The sound doesn't work,' said Lorna. Now fully dressed, she was searching for her uniform in the wardrobe.

'Seldom and a big group of mathematicians were coming back from Cambridge by bus this afternoon,' I said.

Lorna turned round, as if gripped by a terrible foreboding, and came over to me.

'My God, they would have had to cross that bridge if they were coming from there.'

We stared despairingly at the screen. There was a shot of broken glass scattered over the bridge at the spot where the bus had crashed through the barrier. As the reporter peered over the side and pointed, we saw, magnified by the telephoto lens, the mass of crumpled metal that had once been the bus. The camera moved unsteadily, following the reporter as she made her way down the steep slope. A section of the chassis had broken off where the bus must have first struck the ground. The camera swung to show the bottom of the slope, much closer now. Ambulances had managed to reach the bus from below and paramedics had started rescuing passengers. There was a heart-rending close-up of the silent, shattered bus windows and a section of orange bodywork showing an emblem I didn't recognise. Lorna squeezed my arm.

'It's a school bus,' she said. 'My God, there were children inside! Do you think . . . ?' she whispered, unable to finish her sentence. She looked at me, frightened, as if a game we'd been playing had become nightmarish reality. 'I've got to go to the hospital now,' she said, kissing me quickly. 'Just pull the door shut when you leave.'

I sat watching the hypnotic succession of images on the screen. The camera circled the bus, focusing on the window where the rescue team was gathered. A paramedic had managed to climb inside the bus and was trying to get one of the children out. A child's bare legs appeared, swinging disjointedly until a row of arms, forming a stretcher, grabbed hold of them. The child was wearing gym shorts, bloodstained down one side, and bright white trainers. As the rest of his body emerged I saw that he was wearing a vest with a large number across the chest. The camera again focused on the window. A pair of hands was carefully supporting the boy's head. There was blood trickling down the wrists, as if it were pouring from the back of the child's head. The camera showed a close-up of the boy's face and I was startled to see, beneath a long, untidy blond fringe, the unmistakable features of a child with

Down's Syndrome. The face of the man inside the bus now appeared for the first time. He mouthed something, repeating it in desperation and indicating with his bloodstained hands that there was no one left inside the bus.

The camera followed the procession that carried the last child round behind the bus. Someone then stopped the cameraman going any further, but there was a brief glimpse of a row of bodies on stretchers covered with sheets. The programme then returned to the studio and showed a picture of a group of boys before a game. They were the basketball team from a school for children with Down's Syndrome, on their way back from an inter-school competition in Cambridge. The boys' names appeared briefly at the bottom of the screen – five players and five substitutes – followed by the terse statement that all ten were dead. Then another photo appeared: the face of a young man, which I vaguely recognised, though the name beneath the picture, Ralph Johnson, was quite unfamiliar. He was the driver of the bus. He had apparently managed to jump out just before it crashed, but had died too, just before reaching hospital. The photo disappeared from the screen, to be replaced by a list of all the tragedies that had happened at the same spot.

I switched off the television and lay down with a pillow over my eyes, trying to remember where I'd seen the bus driver's face. The picture had no doubt been taken several years earlier. The very short, curly hair, sharp cheekbones, sunken eyes – I'd seen him before, not as a bus driver but somewhere else. Where? I got up irritably and took a long shower, trying to picture all the faces I'd seen around town. As I was dressing and heading back to the bedroom for my shoes, I tried to recall the face on the screen – the small, tight curls, the fanatical expression. Yes. I sat on the bed, stunned by the surprise, by all the different implications. But I was sure I was right. After all, I hadn't met that many people in Oxford. I called the hospital and asked for Lorna. When she came on the phone, I said, automatically lowering my voice:

'The bus driver . . . he was Caitlin's father, wasn't he?'

'Yes,' she said after a moment, and I noticed that she too was almost whispering.

'Is it what I think it is?' I asked.

'I don't know. I didn't want to say anything. One of the lungs was a match. Caitlin's just been taken to theatre – they think they can still save her.'

Chapter 24

'For the first few hours I thought it must have been a mistake,' said Inspector Petersen. 'I thought the real target was the bus you mathematicians were in, which wasn't far behind. I believe some of you even saw the other bus fall down the bank, didn't you?' he asked Seldom.

We were in the French café in Little Clarendon Street. Petersen had arranged to meet us there, away from his office. I wondered if he wanted to apologise, or thank us for something. He was wearing a severe black suit and I remembered that there was to be a special funeral service that morning for the children who had died. It was the first time I'd seen Seldom since his trip to Cambridge. He was grave and silent and the inspector had to repeat his question.

'Yes,' answered Seldom, 'we saw it crash into the barrier and come off the bridge. Our bus stopped immediately and someone called the Radcliffe. Some people thought they could hear screaming from the bottom of the slope. The strange thing is,' he said, as if recounting a nightmare, 'when we looked down, *two ambulances were already there*.'

'They were there because, this time, the message came before, not after the crime. That's the first thing I noticed too. And it didn't go to you, as the previous ones did, but directly to the accident and emergency department at the hospital. They called me as the ambulances set out.'

'What was the message?' I asked.

'"The fourth in the series is the tetraktys. Ten points in the blind triangle." It was a telephone call, and fortunately it was recorded. We've got other recordings of his voice and though he tried to disguise it a bit there's no doubt it's him. We even know where the call was made from: a call box at a service station on the outskirts of Cambridge, where he stopped to fill up with petrol. This is where we find the first intriguing detail. Detective Sergeant Sacks noticed it when he checked the receipts: he bought very little petrol, much less than when leaving Oxford. And sure enough, when we inspected the bus after the crash, we found that the tank was almost empty.'

'He didn't want the bus to catch fire when it crashed,' said Seldom, as if reluctantly agreeing with flawless reasoning.

'Yes,' said Petersen, 'at first I thought that he sent a warning beforehand because unconsciously he wanted us to stop him, or that maybe it was part of the game – he was giving us a handicap. But what he wanted was for the bodies not to be burnt and ambulances to be nearby so that the organs got to the hospital as quickly as possible. He knew that with ten bodies there was a good chance of finding an organ match. I suppose he's won in a way: when we realised what was happening, it was already too late. The transplant was carried out almost immediately, that very afternoon, as soon as they got the consent of the first set of parents, and I'm told the girl is going to live.

'In fact we only started to suspect the father yesterday, when we noticed during a routine check that his name was on the list at Blenheim Palace. He drove a different group of children from the school to the concert. He was supposed to wait for them in the car park. He was in a perfect position to go round the back of the stage, suffocate the percussionist and get back to the car park during all the upheaval without being spotted. At the Radcliffe they confirmed that he knew Mrs Eagleton: a nurse had seen him chatting to her a couple of times. We know too that Mrs Eagleton once had your book on logical series with her in the waiting room. She must have told him you were a friend of hers, not knowing that that would make her the first victim. And lastly, among his books, we found one on the Spartans, one on the Pythagoreans and organ transplants in antiquity, and another on the physical development of children with Down's Syndrome – he wanted to be sure that their lungs could be used.'

'And how did he kill Mr Clarck?' I asked.

'I'll never be able to confirm my theory now, but I don't think Johnson killed Ernest Clarck. He simply waited until a dead body was wheeled out of the ward that he knew Seldom visited. The bodies are left in a little room on that floor, with nobody watching them, sometimes for hours.

All he did was go in and jab the needle of an empty syringe into Clarck's arm, leaving a puncture mark to make it look as if he'd been murdered. In his way, the man truly intended to do as little harm as possible. To understand his reasoning, I think we have to start at the end. I mean, with the group of Down's Syndrome children. He may have begun to have thoughts in that direction when his daughter was refused a lung for the second time. He was still working then, driving the group of Down's Syndrome children to school by bus every morning. He started to think of them as a bank of healthy lungs which he was allowing to get away every day, while his own daughter was dying.

'Repetition leads to desire, and desire leads to obsession. Perhaps at first he thought of killing only one of the children, but he knew it wasn't easy to find a compatible lung. He knew too that many of the parents at the school were devout Catholics. It's very common for parents of such children to turn to religion. Some even believe that their children are angels. He couldn't choose one of the children at random and risk the transplant being refused again, nor could he simply drive the bus off a cliff – the parents would immediately have suspected something and refused to donate organs. It was common knowledge that Ralph Johnson was desperate to save his daughter and that, shortly after she was admitted to hospital, he had checked whether it would be legal for him to donate a lung himself by committing suicide. He needed someone to kill the children for him.

'This was his dilemma until he read, either thanks to Mrs Eagleton, or in the paper, the chapter about serial murders in your book. It gave him the idea he needed. He worked out a plan. It was simple: if he couldn't get some-one to kill the children for him, he'd invent a murderer. An imaginary serial killer who would fool everyone. He'd probably already read about the Pythagoreans, so it was easy for him to come up with a series of symbols that would be seen as a challenge to a mathematician. The second symbol – the fish – might, however, have had an additional private connotation: it was the symbol of the early Christians. It may have been his way of signalling that he was getting his revenge. We know too that he was fascinated by the *tetraktys* symbol – he drew it in the margin of almost all his books – possibly because of its correlation with the number ten, the full basketball team, the number of children he was thinking of killing.

'He chose Mrs Eagleton to start the series because it would be hard to find an easier victim: an elderly lady, an invalid who stayed at home alone in the afternoons. Above all, he didn't want the police to be alerted at the start. This was a key element of his plan. The first murders had to be discreet, imperceptible, so that we wouldn't be on his trail immediately and he'd have time to get to the fourth murder. He only needed one person to know – you. Something went slightly wrong with the first murder but he was still cleverer than us and he didn't make any more mistakes. So, in a way, he won. It's odd, but I can't quite bring myself to condemn him. I too have a daughter. You never know how far you'd go for your child.'

'Do you think he was planning to save himself?' asked Seldom.

'We'll never know,' answered Petersen. 'When the bus was examined, it turned out that the steering had been

180

tampered with. In theory, that would have given him an alibi. On the other hand, he could have jumped from the bus sooner. I think he wanted to stay at the wheel as long as possible, to make sure the bus fell down the slope. He only jumped once it had crashed through the barrier. He was unconscious when they found him and he died in the ambulance on the way to the hospital.' The inspector glanced at his watch and beckoned to a waiter. 'Right, I don't want to be late for the service. I'd just like to say again how much I've appreciated your help, both of you.' And he smiled openly at Seldom for the first time. 'I read as much as I could of the books you lent me, but maths was never my strong point.'

We stood and watched him head towards St Giles's Church, where a large crowd was already gathered. There were a few women in black veils, and some had to be helped up the front steps and into the church.

'Are you going back to the Institute?' asked Seldom.

'Yes,' I said. 'In fact I shouldn't have taken any time off now: I've got to finish and post my grant report without fail today. And you?'

'Me?' he said. He glanced in the direction of the church and, for a moment, he seemed very alone and strangely helpless. 'I think I'll wait here until the service is over. I'd like to follow the procession to the cemetery.'

Chapter 25

I spent the next few hours, stumbling more and more often, like a tired hurdler, as I filled in a series of ridiculous boxes on my report form. At last, at four o'clock, I printed up the files and slipped the pages into a large manila envelope. I went down to the secretary's office, asked Kim to make sure it was posted to Argentina that afternoon and left the building feeling slightly euphoric at my liberation.

On my way back to Cunliffe Close, I remembered that I had to pay Beth my second month's rent, so I made a slight detour to get money from a cash machine. I found myself retracing the route of a month earlier, at almost exactly the same hour. The afternoon air was just as warm, the streets just as quiet. Everything seemed to be repeating itself, as if I were being given a last opportunity to go back to the day when everything started. I decided to walk along the same side of Banbury Road – the side in the sun – brushing past privet hedges, submitting to the mysterious conjunction of repetitions. When I reached the turning of Cunliffe Close I saw the last shred of the badger's skin still lying in the road. That hadn't been there a month earlier. I forced myself to look at it. The passing cars, the rain, dogs, had all done their work. There was no blood left, just a last piece of fur-covered skin, like a strip of dried-out peel. A badger will do anything to save its young, Beth had said. Hadn't I heard something similar that morning? Yes, Inspector Petersen had said, 'You never know how far you'd go for your child.' I stood frozen, my eyes glued to that last remnant, listening in the silence. Suddenly, I knew. I saw, as if it had always been there, what it was that Seldom had wanted me to see from the start. *He'd told me*, almost letter by letter, but I hadn't listened. He'd repeated it, a hundred different ways. He'd put the photographs under my nose but all I'd seen were M's, hearts and eights.

I turned round and walked back up Banbury Road, impelled by a single thought: I had to find Seldom. I went through the market and along the High, then cut through a passage to get to Merton as quickly as possible. But Seldom wasn't there. I stood for a moment at the window of the porter's lodge, slightly disorientated. I asked if Seldom had come back at lunchtime but nobody remembered seeing him since first thing that morning. It suddenly occurred to me that he might be at the hospital, visiting Frank Kalman. I had a few coins in my pocket so I called Lorna from the pay phone in the college and asked her to put me through to the second floor. No, Mr Kalman hadn't had any visitors.

'Can you think where else Seldom might be?' I asked Lorna when I was transferred back to her.

There was a silence at the other end of the line. I couldn't tell if she was just thinking, or trying to decide whether to tell me something that would reveal the true nature of the relationship she'd had with Seldom.

'What's the date today?' she asked unexpectedly.

It was the twenty-fifth of June. Lorna sighed, as if in agreement.

'It's the day his wife died, the day of the accident. I think you'll find him at the Ashmolean Museum.'

I walked back up Magdalen Street and climbed the steps to the museum. This was my first visit. I crossed a small gallery of portraits, presided over by the inscrutable face of John Dee, and followed the signs to the great Assyrian frieze. Seldom was the only person in the room. He was sitting on one of the stools that were set out at a certain distance from the central wall. As I moved closer I saw that the frieze extended, like a long, slender stone parchment, all around the room. Involuntarily, I trod more quietly as I approached Seldom. He was fully absorbed, his eyes, empty of all expression, fixed on a detail of the frieze, as if he had long before stopped seeing it. For a moment I wondered if I shouldn't wait for him outside. When he turned towards me he showed no surprise. He said simply, in his usual unassuming tone:

'If you're here, it's because you know, or because you think you know. Isn't that so? Take a seat,' he said, indicating the stool beside him. 'If you want to see the entire frieze you have to sit here.'

I sat down and saw a succession of multicoloured images of what appeared to be an immense battlefield. Small figures were carved into the golden stone with wonderful precision. In scene after scene a single warrior appeared to

184

confront an entire army. He was recognisable by his long beard and a sword that stood out from the rest. When I looked along the frieze from left to right, the endlessly repeated image of the warrior produced a vivid impression of movement. Looking again, I noticed that the different successive positions of the warrior could be seen as a progression in time and that, at the end of the frieze, there were many more fallen figures, as if he had defeated the whole army single-handed.

'King Nissam, eternal warrior,' said Seldom, his voice sounding strange. 'That's the name with which the frieze was presented to King Nissam and with which it arrived at the British Museum three thousand years later. But the stone guards a different story for whoever has the patience to see it. My wife managed to reconstruct almost all of it when the frieze came here. If you read the sign over there you'll see that the most important Assyrian sculptor, a man called Hassiri, was commissioned to produce the work, to celebrate the king's birthday. Hassiri had a son, Nemrod, to whom he'd taught his art, who worked with him. Nemrod was engaged to a very young girl, Agartis. On the same day that father and son were preparing the stone before starting the work, King Nissam, out hunting, came upon the girl by the river. He tried to take her by force but Agartis, who had not recognised the king, tried to escape into the forest. The king caught her easily: he raped her and then cut off her head with his sword. When he returned to the palace and passed the sculptors, father and son caught sight of the girl's head hanging from the saddle with the rest of the catch from the hunt. Hassiri went to tell the girl's mother the terrible news.

'His son meanwhile, in despair, began carving into the stone the figure of the king cutting off a kneeling woman's head. On his return, Hassiri found his son dementedly hammering an image into the stone that would surely condemn him to death. He dragged him away from the wall, sent him home and remained alone with his dilemma. He could easily have erased the image. But Hassiri was an artist in antiquity and he believed that every work of art contained a mysterious truth protected by a divine hand, a truth that men had no right to destroy. Perhaps too, as much as his son, he wanted future generations to know what happened. That night he hung a cloth over the wall and asked to be left alone to work in secret, hidden beneath the cloth. The frieze he was preparing, he said, would be quite different from all his previous work, and the king should be the first to look upon it.

'Alone with that first image in the stone, Hassiri was in the same dilemma as the general in G.K. Chesterton's "The Sign of the Broken Sword": where does a wise man hide a pebble? On the beach, of course. But what does he do if there is no beach? And where does a man hide a dead soldier? On a battlefield, of course. But what if there is no battle? A general can start a battle, and a sculptor can . . . imagine one. King Nissam, eternal warrior, never took part in a battle; he lived during an unusually peaceful era and probably only ever killed unarmed women in his lifetime. Though the king found the war theme a little surprising, the frieze was flattering to him and he thought it a good idea to exhibit it in the palace so as to intimidate neighbouring kings. Nissam, and countless generations after him, saw only what the artist wanted them to see: an overwhelming succession of images from which the viewer soon looks away, believing he finds repetition, that he has understood the rule, that each part represents the whole. That's the trap created by the recurrence of the figure with the sword. But there is a tiny hidden part which contradicts and cancels out the rest, a part which is in itself another whole. I didn't have to wait as long as Hassiri. I too wanted someone, at least one other person, to find out. I wanted someone to know the truth and judge. I suppose I should be pleased you've seen it at last.'

Seldom stood and opened the window behind me before starting to roll a cigarette. Seemingly reluctant to sit down again, he continued to stand as he went on:

'That first afternoon, when we met, I had received a message – not from a stranger or a madman but from someone, unfortunately, very close to me. It was a confession to a crime and a desperate plea for help. The note was in my pigeonhole, as I told Inspector Petersen, when I went to my class, but I only took it out and read it on my way down to the cafeteria, an hour later. I went straight to Cunliffe Close, where I bumped into you at the front door. I still thought there might be an element of exaggeration in the message. *I've done something terrible*, it said. But I still never would have imagined what we found. Someone you've cradled in your arms when she was a little girl is always a little girl to you. I'd always protected her. I wouldn't have been capable of calling the police. I suppose if I'd been at the house alone I'd have tried to remove clues, clean up the blood, hide the pillow. But you were there, so I had to make the call. I'd read about Inspector Petersen's cases, and I knew that as soon as he was in charge and on her trail she'd be finished.

'While we waited for the police to arrive, I was in the same dilemma as Hassiri. Where does a wise man hide a pebble? On a beach. Where does one hide a figure holding a sword? On a battlefield. And where does one hide a murder? It could no longer be hidden in the past. The answer was simple, if horrific: there only remained the future, it could only be hidden in a series of murders. After my book came out, I received letters from all manner of deranged people. There was one in particular who claimed he killed a homeless man every time his bus ticket had a prime number. I had no trouble inventing a murderer who left a symbol from a logical series at every murder scene, like a challenge. I wasn't prepared to *commit* murder, of course and I wasn't sure how I'd resolve that, but I didn't have time to think about it. When the police pathologist established that the time of death was between two and three in the afternoon, I realised they'd arrest her immediately, so I decided to take a leap in the dark.

'The piece of paper I'd thrown in my bin that afternoon was the rough draft of a proof in which I'd made an error but then wanted to retrieve. I was sure that Brent would remember the paper if the police asked him about it. I thought up a brief message, like the details for an appointment. I had to provide her with an alibi, so the most important thing was the time. I chose three in the afternoon, the latest time of death given by the pathologist. I knew that she was in rehearsal by then. When the inspector asked me if there was anything else in the note, I remembered that you and I had been speaking in Spanish and that when I'd glanced at the letters on the Scrabble racks I'd seen the word "*aro*", or circle in Spanish. The circle was in fact the symbol I suggested in my book as the start of a series with maximum uncertainty.'

'"*Aro*",' I said. 'That's what you wanted me to see in the photos.'

'Yes. I tried to tell you every way I could think of. You're not English, so you're the only person who could have formed the word out of the letters on the rack and read it as I had. As we walked to the Sheldonian after giving our statements, I tried to find out if you'd noticed that or any other detail I might have missed and that could have implicated her. You drew my attention to the final position of the head, eyes facing the back of the chaise longue. She confessed to me later that she hadn't been able to stand the fixed stare of those eyes.'

'Why did you hide the blanket?'

'At the theatre, I asked her to tell me everything, step by step, exactly as it happened. That's why I insisted on going to give her the news myself: I wanted to make sure she spoke to me before she had to face the police. I had to tell her about my plan and I wanted, above all, to find out if she'd been careless about anything else. She told me she'd worn her evening gloves so as not to leave fingerprints but that she had, indeed, had to struggle with her and had torn the blanket with the heel of her shoe. She thought the police might guess the murderer was a woman because of that. She still had the blanket in her bag, so we agreed that I'd get rid of it. She was extremely agitated and I was sure she'd break down as soon as Petersen started questioning her. I knew that if the inspector focused his investigation on her she'd be finished. And I knew that to lodge the serial murder theory in his mind I'd have to provide him with a second murder as soon as possible. Fortunately, in our first conversation, *you* had given me the idea that I needed, when we talked about imperceptible murders – murders that nobody saw as murders. A truly imperceptible murder, I realised, didn't even have to be a murder.

'I thought immediately of Frank's ward. I saw corpses wheeled out of there every day. I simply needed to get hold of a syringe and, as Petersen guessed, wait patiently for the first dead body to be placed in the little room off the main corridor. It was a Sunday, and Beth was away on tour. It was perfect for her. I checked the time of death noted on the label, to make sure that I too had an alibi, and then stuck the needle into the corpse's arm, just to leave a puncture mark. That was as far as I was prepared to go. When I was researching unsolved murders, I'd read that forensic pathologists had for some time suspected that there existed a chemical that was dissipated within a few hours without leaving any trace. That suspicion was enough for me. And anyway, my murderer had supposedly planned things carefully enough to outsmart the police as well. I had already decided that the second symbol would be the fish, and that the series would be the first few Pythagorean numbers.

'From the hospital I went straight to the Institute and stuck a note similar to the one I described to Petersen on the revolving door. The inspector pieced that part of it together and I think I was a suspect for a time. It was after the second death that Sacks started following me.'

'But you couldn't have done anything at the concert – you were sitting next to me!' I said.

'The concert . . . The concert was the first sign of what I most feared, the nightmare that has haunted me since childhood. In accordance with my plan, I was waiting for a car accident, in exactly the spot that Johnson chose to crash off the road. It was where I had my accident, and was the only thing I could think of for the third symbol in the series, the triangle. I thought I would send a note after the event, claiming an ordinary everyday car accident as a murder, a perfect murder that leaves no clues. That was my choice and it would have been the last death. Straight after, I intended to publicise the solution to the series which I myself had initiated. My imaginary intellectual opponent would admit defeat and either disappear quietly, or leave behind a few false trails so that the police would continue chasing a ghost a little longer. But then the man died at the concert.

'It was what I was looking for – a death. From where we were sitting it really did look like someone was strangling him. It was easy to believe we were witnessing a murder. But perhaps the most extraordinary thing was that the dead man had been playing the triangle. I took it as a good omen, as if my plan had been approved at a higher sphere and life was making things easy for me. As I've said, I've never known how to read the signs in the real world. I thought I could appropriate the percussionist's death for my plan. While you and the others rushed towards the stage, I checked that nobody was looking and tore out of the programme the two words that I needed for my message. Then I simply placed them on my seat and followed you. Later, when the inspector motioned to us and made his way along our row, I stopped deliberately, as if stunned, just before reaching my seat, so that he would be the one to pick up the words. That was the little illusion I created. Of course, fate had – or so I assumed – given me an extraordinary helping hand, because even Petersen was there to witness events. The doctor who went up on stage confirmed what had been obvious to me: it was a natural respiratory arrest, despite its dramatic appearance. I would have been surprised had the post-mortem revealed anything strange.

'My only remaining problem – which I had already solved once – was making a natural death look like murder, and providing a convincing theory so that Petersen would include the death as one of the series. It was more difficult this time, because I couldn't get near the body and put my hands around the neck. I then remembered the case of the telepath. All I could come up with was to suggest that it was a case of remote hypnosis. But I knew that it would be almost impossible to convince Petersen, even if he still had doubts about Mrs Crafford's death. It wasn't, so to speak, within the aesthetic of his reasoning, in the realm of the probable. He wouldn't have thought it a plausible theory, as we would say in mathematics. But in the end none of it proved necessary. Petersen easily accepted a theory that, to me, seemed much more flimsy, that the man was attacked from behind. He accepted it, even though he himself was there and saw the same as us: that for all the theatricality of the death, there was no one else there. He accepted it for the reason people usually believe things: because he *wanted* to believe.

'Perhaps the strangest thing is that Petersen didn't even consider the possibility that it might have been a natural death. I realised that though he may have had doubts before, he was now quite convinced that he was pursuing a serial killer, so it seemed perfectly reasonable to find murders at every turn, even on the one evening he was at a concert with his daughter.'

'Don't you think Johnson could have attacked the percussionist, as Petersen believes?' I asked.

'No, I don't think so. That's only possible if you follow Petersen's line of argument. In other words, if Johnson had also planned the deaths of Mrs Eagleton and Ernest Clarck. But up until the evening of the concert it would have been very difficult for Johnson to make the correct connection between those two first deaths. I think, that evening, that Johnson, like me, misread the sign. He may not even have witnessed the man's death, since he was supposed to stay and wait for the children on the bus. But he must have seen the story in the paper the following day. He saw the series of symbols, a series to which he knew the continuation. He'd read fanatically about the Pythagoreans and felt, like me, that his plan was being approved at a higher sphere. The number of children in the basketball team was the same as the number of points in the *tetraktys*. His daughter had been given barely forty-eight hours to live. Everything seemed to be saying: this is your chance, your last chance. That's what I tried to explain to you that day in the park, the nightmare that's haunted me since I was a child – the consequences, the endless derivations, the monsters conjured by the mind. All I wanted was to make sure she didn't go to prison and now I'm responsible for the deaths of eleven people.'

He was silent a moment, staring out of the window.

'All this time you've been my yardstick. I knew that if I

could convince you about the series, I'd be able to convince Petersen. I also knew that if I'd missed something, you might point it out to me. But I also wanted to be fair, if that's the right word here – to give you every opportunity to discover the truth. How did you realise in the end?' he asked suddenly.

'I remembered what Inspector Petersen said this morning: that you never know how far a father will go for his child. The day I saw you and Beth together in the market I thought I sensed a strange relationship between you. I was particularly intrigued by the fact that she seemed to want your approval for her marriage. I wondered if you could really have invented a series of murders to shield someone you didn't even see that often.'

'Yes, even in despair she knew exactly where to turn. I don't know whether what she believes is true and I suppose I never will. I don't know what her mother told her about us. She'd never mentioned it to me before. But perhaps to make sure I'd help her, she played her trump card.' From the inside pocket of his jacket he took a piece of paper folded in four and handed it to me. 'I've done something terrible,' read the first line, in a strangely childish hand. The second line, which looked as if it had been added in desperation, said, in large anguished letters: 'Please, please, you have to help me, Daddy.'

Epilogue

As I came down the steps of the museum, the sun was still there, with the benign, extended brightness of late afternoons in summer. I walked back to Cunliffe Close, leaving behind the golden cupola of the Observatory. As I made my way slowly up Banbury Road, I wondered what to do with the confession I had just heard. Lights were coming on in a few houses and through the windows I glimpsed bags of shopping, televisions playing – fragments of normal life proceeding unperturbed behind the hedges. In Rawlinson Road a car, behind me, honked twice briefly and cheerfully. I turned round, expecting to see Lorna. Instead I found Beth waving from a small, brand-new, metallic-blue convertible. I went to the kerb. She smoothed her untidy hair and leaned across the passenger seat, smiling broadly.

'Would you like a lift?'

She stretched out a hand to open the door, but she must have seen something odd in my expression because the hand stopped midway. I complimented her mechanically on her new car and then looked into her eyes. I looked as if I were seeing her for the first time and ought to find something new in her. But she was happier, more carefree, more beautiful, that was all.

'Is something wrong?' she asked. 'Where have you been?'

'I've just been speaking to Arthur Seldom,' I answered hesitantly.

A look of alarm flashed across her eyes.

'About maths?' she asked.

'No,' I said. 'We were talking about the murders. He told me everything.'

Her face darkened and she placed both hands on the wheel, her body suddenly tense.

'Everything? No, I don't think he can have told you everything.' She smiled anxiously to herself and the old bitterness appeared in her eyes for a moment. 'He could never bring himself to tell you *everything*. But I see,' she said, glancing at me again cautiously, 'that you believe him. What are you going to do?'

'Nothing. What can I do? They'd probably arrest him too,' I said, staring at her. Of all the questions, there was really only one I wanted to ask. I leaned towards her and looked into her hard blue eyes. 'What made you do it?'

'What made you come here?' she asked. 'You didn't come just to study maths, did you? Why did you choose Oxford?' A slow tear appeared on her eyelashes. 'It was something you said. The day I saw you getting out of that car with your tennis racket, looking so happy. When we talked about grants. "You should try it," you said. I couldn't stop repeating it to myself: *you should try it*. I thought she was going to die soon and I'd have a chance to start a new life. But a few days later she got her test results. The cancer was in remission, the doctor told her she might live another ten years. Another ten years shackled to that old witch . . . I couldn't bear it.'

The tear on her lashes now rolled down her cheek. She wiped it away abruptly, self-consciously, and searched for a tissue in the glove compartment. When she placed her hands back on the wheel I again noticed her small thumb.

'So, are you getting in?'

'Next time,' I said. 'It's a lovely afternoon, I'd like to walk a little further.'

She drove off and I watched the car grow smaller until it disappeared into Cunliffe Close. I wondered if what Beth thought Seldom would never dare tell me was what he had already told me, or whether there was something else, something I didn't dare imagine. I wondered how much of the truth I really knew and where to start when writing my second report. At the beginning of Cunliffe Close, I looked down but could see no sign of the badger. The last shred of flesh had disappeared, and as far as the eye could see, the road stretching ahead of me was clean, clear, innocent once more.

A FLORENTINE DEATH

Michele Giuttari

Meet Michele Ferrara. Lover of a good bottle of local Rossi di Montalcino, smoker of Antico Toscano cigars – and head of Florence's elite police force, the squadra mobile. With a rising murder rate and high levels of Mafia activity, Ferrara has an unenviable job. And when a spate of brutal murders strikes Florence, Ferrara's role becomes even more dangerous. It seems that a serial killer is at work, killing one man in a shop selling religious artefacts, another in a quiet antiques showroom. With sick, teasing notes arriving for him from the killer, Ferrara needs to solve the crime before he becomes the next victim.

The gripping and cleverly plotted first novel by real-life police chief Michele Giuttari, *A Florentine Death* offers a fascinating insight into both the beauty and the darkness of Florence.

'Has all the hallmarks of becoming a classic of the genre –
a highly atmospheric tale of murder, the mafia and the
rarely explored criminal underbelly of Florentine life . . .
Ferrara is set to run and run'
Daily Mirror

'An exceptional thriller and I'd wager a handy sum that
Michele Ferrara will be with us for some time to come'
Evening Herald

Abacus
978-0-349-12005-8

THE ATHENIAN MURDERS

José Carlos Somoza

When the body of a young man is discovered on the slopes of Mount Lycabettus, it is initially assumed that a pack of wolves is responsible for his death. But Tramachus, an aspiring student at Plato's academy, has been murdered and Heracles Pontor, known as the 'Decipherer of Enigmas', is called in to help unravel the truth.

Meanwhile, in the footnotes of *The Athenian Murders*, a second story is emerging. The modern-day translator realises that there is a message hidden in the images of the original narrative. And the more he translates, the more the clues pull together to reveal an astonishing truth, one that bears an eerie resemblance to his own life . . .

'Extremely subtle and intelligent . . . totally absorbing'
Evening Standard

'A thriller of great originality, with a detective
in Heracles to rival Chief Inspector Morse as
one of the cleverest in crime fiction'
Sunday Telegraph

Abacus
978-0-349-11618-1

THE ART OF MURDER

José Carlos Somoza

Murder is not a science. It's an art form.

Welcome to an art scene where realism has gone one step further, where each painting is literally alive, where the model for each masterpiece is the canvas itself. And for the beautiful men and women queuing up for the privilege – to be painted and posed, bought and rented by collectors – there is one artist they are all drawn to: the mysterious Dutch master, Bruno van Tysch.

Then a young female model, Annek Hollech, is abducted and killed, viciously murdered in a most gruesome fashion. The detectives assigned to the case, April Wood and Lothar Bosch, may have little interest in modem art, but they are going to have to acquire an appreciation extremely quickly. Because van Tysch is about to launch a major exhibition in Amsterdam – the imitation of thirteen of Rembrandt's masterpieces – and the rumours are that the killer is about to strike again . . .

Abacus
978-0-349-11883-3

Now you can order superb titles directly from Abacus

☐	A Florentine Death	Michele Giuttari	£10.99
☐	The Athenian Murders	José Carlos Somoza	£7.99
☐	The Art of Murder	José Carlos Somoza	£7.99

The prices shown above are correct at time of going to press. However, the publishers reserve the right to increase prices on covers from those previously advertised, without further notice.

──────────────── ⟨ABACUS⟩ ────────────────

Please allow for postage and packing: **Free UK delivery.**
Europe: add 25% of retail price; Rest of World: 45% of retail price.

To order any of the above or any other Abacus titles, please call our credit card orderline or fill in this coupon and send/fax it to:

Abacus, PO Box 121, Kettering, Northants NN14 4ZQ
Fax: 01832 733076   Tel: 01832 737527
Email: aspenhouse@FSBDial.co.uk

☐ I enclose a UK bank cheque made payable to Abacus for £ . . . .
☐ Please charge £ . . . . . . to my Visa/Delta/Maestro

☐☐☐☐☐☐☐☐☐☐☐☐☐☐☐☐☐☐☐

Expiry Date ☐☐☐☐   Maestro Issue No. ☐☐

NAME (BLOCK LETTERS please) . . . .

ADDRESS . . . .

. . . .

. . . .

Postcode . . . . Telephone . . . .

Signature . . . .

Please allow 28 days for delivery within the UK. Offer subject to price and availability.

Please do not send any further mailings from companies carefully selected by Abacus ☐